Life Ain't Nothing But a

Holey Holy Riddle

By

John Polodna

Holey Holy Riddle is a totally fictional story, and any resemblance to any living persons or situations is coincidental.

Polodna Publishing
2440 Markridge Circle
Racine, Wisconsin 53405

Dedication and Acknowledgements

This is dedicated to all my family, immediate and extended, here and in the here after. I value each and every one of you.

The first person to take a strong and serious interest in this project was my brother David. He provided me with a computer, technical support, editing services and loads of moral support. After reading the first very rough draft he said, "You must get this published."

My father-in-law, Warren Miller, was persuaded to read an early manuscript and has read it in several draft forms. He provided the inspiration that lead to Chapter Three, and many other suggestions that made a qualitative difference.

My writer's group, especially Pat Fitzgerald, Darin Zimpel, and Dodie Kovac slogged through the manuscript line by line making many valuable suggestions. Then Dodie took on this story as a special project and donated an untold number of hours proof reading and editing the final manuscript. Her corrections and suggestions were very valuable.

My wife Jane was there for me in the beginning, throughout, and at the end: supporting, proof reading and editing. In the middle of keeping our real world afloat she was asked hundreds of questions about my make-believe world of Marion and Davie.

Since this story leans very heavily on country music, I want to express the keen sadness we all feel at the recent passing of Johnny Cash and June Carter Cash just four months apart.

May 29, 2005

Life Ain't Nothing But a

Holey Holy Riddle

TO Jon + Steanie
Thanks!!

John Polodna

Copyright © 2003
by
John Polodna

All rights reserved. No part of this book may be reproduced in any form, except for the inclusion of brief quotations in a review, without permission in writing from the author.

ISBN: 0-9745981-0-0

Library of Congress Control Number: 2003097787

Printed in the United States by
Morris Publishing
3212 East Highway 30
Kearney, NE 68847
1-800-650-7888

Table of Contents

Chapter   Page

1. Marion Hensley 1
2. Oct. 16, 1997   Green Bay, WI 11
3. Sept. 3, 1997   Rome, Italy 20

4. Oct. 22, 1997   Green Bay, WI 32
5. Oct. 25, 1997   Green Bay, WI 37
6. Oct. 28, 1997   Austin, Texas 42

7. Nov. 5, 1997   Green Bay, WI 54
8. Nov. 6, 1997   Green Bay, WI 57
9. Dec. 10, 1997   Green Bay, WI 65

10. Jan. 9, 1998   Green Bay, WI 74
11. Jan. 14, 1998   Green Bay, WI 82
12. Feb. 2, 1998   Green Bay, WI 90

13. April 15, 1998   San Antonio 96
14. May 13, 1998   Austin, Texas 104
15. June 18, 1998   Austin, Texas 113

16. June 19, 1998   Austin, Texas 133
17. June 20, 1998   Austin, Texas 141
18. Benediction   Austin, Texas 169
19. Oct. 18, 1998   Green Bay, WI 173

Holey Holy Riddle
Chapter One
Marion Hensley

My earliest memory is of kindergarten, and wondering why my mother was leaving her darling little girl alone with so many strange and noisy children. I remember my sheer panic that first day of school when she took me there then turned around and left. It seemed like there were hundreds of the little savages, and they were so messy. During the May Day celebration that year all of us kindergartners were part of a little parade in front of the school. My mother sent me to school in this girlie-girl dress, which she did most of the time anyway up until fourth grade. About half way through the parade I felt something in the back of my dress. I looked around and saw nothing but the sensation didn't go away. I kept feeling around on the back of my dress but I was way too shy to say anything to the teacher. It worried me the rest of the day. That afternoon, when I got home from school, I locked myself in the bathroom and undressed. There in the back of my dress was a squished bee that I must have killed in my searching.

In grade school I kept growing and growing until I was taller than any of my classmates. The boys would call me beanpole or beanstalk. That was so embarrassing. You know those games that grade schoolers play: girls chase boys and boys chase girls. At first I didn't get chased at all until this new boy Dino Bina, came to school. He chased me one time and I smacked him solidly in the kisser. He didn't return to school until the next week, and the teacher kept us in the next day at recess and lectured us about how to play nicely together.

When I was a teenager the thought of boys, dating and all that slobbery stuff scared me so much that I sometimes showered in my nightgown. My parents wanted me to be a cheerleader and get straight As. The studies were easy enough for me, but getting Cs was a good way to go unnoticed. The closest that I came to cheerleading was singing baritone in the back row of the high school chorus. It wasn't until my class took a Health Science course in high school that I learned that I was shy or introverted, as the book would say. I sure didn't get it from my mother because she was such a talker. Always bragging on her little Marion this and her little Marion that. Anybody could hear her a block away. No, I got it from my dad. Then I started observing him. Dad had a way of dealing with his shyness and, you might say, making conversation. He had these ten jokes and stories that he would tell over and over. He even gave himself three to four seconds of laughter after each joke, every time.

After high school I attended Northeast Wisconsin Technical School, and continued to live at home. My major was

Business Administration, which I figured would keep me busy with laws and numbers and away from belligerent kids and drooling men. One of my teachers was a severely anorexic bitterly listless woman named Mrs. Roberts. Many years later, I learned through the grapevine that she interpreted my shyness as being snobbery. I worked as hard as I could and never got more than a B from her. After graduation I had three very hot possibilities. My first love was to go to work for Northwestern Mutual Life Insurance, as they had promised me a totally backroom position dealing only with files and figures. My source told me that Mrs. Roberts then interceded with the Northwestern interviewer and revealed secrets about my personality. There was no second interview and no job. Luckily I didn't know that then; maybe I'd have smacked her in the kisser!

So, I ended up at the bank and they wouldn't let me start in the backroom. Working at the bank got me talking to a lot of different people, if you know what I mean, different. First I was a teller, then a Special Customer Assistant. And because I was working at the bank I met Davie Fender, a real people magnet; a man with merriment on his face and music in his soul. Davie and I started dating, even though he was forty-five years old, which made him sixteen years older than this banker chick. He gives me enormous confidence; so much that telling this story would be impossible without him. But, you aren't going to hear any of the juicy stuff from me. You'll have to watch *The Phil Donahue Show* for that.

Well, it's easier telling you about Roy and Michael before talking about my Davie. Michael and Davie are the house band at Roy's bar, which he calls a cultural vessel and first class saloon. Roy is always dreaming and scheming to make his establishment the next Microsoft of country music. One night he held a mud-wrestling contest while the boys were on break. What a mess. There was mud everywhere. Davie was cleaning the sludge out of the instruments for the next month. Michael was furious and threatened to quit if Roy persisted with his inane promotions. There was also plenty of mud left on the dance floor. During the next set there were line dancers flying everywhere, and their screams are still echoing through town. Davie calls them Roy's get poor quick schemes. But, just between you and me, I know Roy has plenty of money.

There must be a dozen different stories about how Davie and Michael met. Of course, Roy tells the most colorful ones. They all agree it had something to do with the Twin Forty Three Drive In Movie Theater. When he was fifteen years old, Davie started carrying his guitar with him everywhere he went. Davie's version of the story is pretty lame and goes something like this. One night he met Michael and Valerie at the drive in and he crooned them a tune. Because of Davie's singing to them, their friendship burst into a Debbie Reynold's romance, and immediately after high school they became engaged. Makes you a little sick, doesn't it? I know it's even too syrupy for me to swallow. Listening to Michael tell the story of their meeting has a completely different twist. Because of his high school celebrity status Davie thought he could get away with anything.

One night at the drive in, guitar and all, he approached the car belonging to the meanest jock in the county. With the aim of playing this rowdy and his date a tune, he opened the car door. It was the most inopportune time. The bruiser sprung from the car, destroyed the guitar and was about to destroy Davie. Luckily, Michael Vaughn came along and saved him. I like that version, and it's probably closer to the truth. Because when Davie is around stuff just happens.

You might say Michael is really different from his family. Davie calls it the mailman effect. But seriously, his family are just nine-to-five people. Not Michael. He can play umpteen instruments and even played the tuba in the Green Bay High School marching band. Michael has two sisters and Davie was an only child, so they are sometimes closer than brothers. Since their days as The Book of Joshua, their first duo, they've been together. At the time Davie was attending St. Norbert's, a private Catholic school, and they played mainly for friends. Their next band included a couple of other guys and was called Buzzards by The Bay. That's when Davie started experimenting with twang and found out he had some natural ability for that twang thang. Then by sending away to Nashville, he got a record of 101 Twangs. After all of these years he still has it. None of his ex-wives wanted it.

You have to know one thing about these three guys. They badger and bicker all of the time, but they really like each other. There's something about the Green Bay natives. It's like an invisible umbilical cord runs through all of them. Now, take Gina Bina from Neenah. She moved here when she was three months old, and nobody treats her like a native. Vince Lombardi was an okay coach, but he wasn't a native. And that cracker jack piano player from Georgia, Johnny Lee Linton, he definitely wasn't a native. He arrived when the Fort Harold Paper Company transferred his dad here. There was always this competitive thing between him and Davie. Who would want to be named Johnny Lee and living in Green Bay? Thank goodness I'm a native. I was the most bashful. Oh, that's not important now.

Well, I guess it's time to tell you about the love of my life. Roy calls him my weathered leathered hombre. He didn't always look that way. The first time I saw Davie Fender; he was the sleekest thing in the world to this demure nineteen-year-old. A couple of friends from the Technical School talked me into going to Appleton where he and Michael were appearing in the classy ballroom of the plush Paper Valley Inn. They attracted such a multitude of music lovers, a couple of hundred hot fans squeezed together in a steamy swarm, because Davie was such an incredible performer. That night he was strutting across the stage while wailing on his fiddle and never missing a note. They blended Davie's twang and Michael's bass to create the most furored melodies. I was so excited that my passions were ready to explode. But, I didn't. I saw them in concert a few more times, but it always took me a month to depressurize. Many years later I found out that during the 1970s and 80s he and Michael were performing like that twice a week.

Davie's mother, Helen, was not a native and was considered to be eccentric. She really wasn't that unconventional, but this is Green Bay where bell-bottom trousers are considered to be eccentric. She gave all of the natives something to talk about. Helen met Otto, Davie's dad, when he was running his first used car lot in the city. Some of Otto's friends advised him about taking up with a person like Helen, being that she was a high school music teacher. Davie's parents are gone now, but from my vantage point, they had an outstanding marriage. They were always in a tug of war over Davie's soul, his mother with the music and his dad with the business. She would entertain toddler Davie for hours by playing their old Glen Miller and Guy Lombardo records. She was thrilled to see him have such interest at such a young age. He'd heartily sing along with Bing Crosby performing *Home On The Range*. By the age of six he was eagerly following her lead in plinking out *Twinkle Twinkle Little Star* on the piano.

Being financed by a father who owned Fender Ford, the largest dealership in the area, Davie grew up wanting for nothing. You wouldn't know it now with him driving around in an eight year old Tempo. Otto supported his son in everything. He paid for private music lessons with the best teachers around. He bought him expensive instruments and he even replaced the guitar that was destroyed at the drive in. Otto wanted Davie to follow him into the automobile business and some day take over the dealership. Right after high school he started Davie as a salesman. The ole country star could charm the customers all right. But this gig only lasted a year as Davie would usually show up for work late, hung over or both. Completing the required paper work that went along with selling a car was a mystery as deep as quantum physics for Davie. Then he quit the church. Otto was a strong man of the church, first lay reader at St. Joseph's, and all of this tested him severely. All that Otto could see was Davie's continual downward spiral into country music. His pride was hurt too often.

At the same time, Michael and Valerie had just gotten married. Maki, a nickname that Davie coined for his best friend because it rhymes with wacky, was working at Miller's Music Store during the day and taking classes at night. Davie had created Green Bay Boogie, a red-hot country swing band, with Michael and two other musicians. Maki was exhausted all of the time and Davie was smoking too much rope. Otherwise, "these were the best of times," as some famous writer once said.

Unexpectedly, the Miller Music Store came up for sale and Maki wanted to buy it. Like most young men his age, he didn't have the cash to make it happen. Michael talked to several people around town about helping him finance the music store. After they turned him down he ended up talking to Davie's dad. Otto had always been impressed with Michael's serious nature. Unfortunately, Davie and his dad were barely speaking at the time. Otto agreed to loan Michael the money he needed to buy the music store. Davie was jealous and furious. He disbanded Green Bay Boogie and didn't hide his displeasure with Michael. That left Michael with the music store and Davie with nothing. Trying to relaunch his star, he played some solo gigs and drank plenty of booze. He also tried catching on with some other bands, but mainly floundered around for a couple of years. Finally he approached Michael about getting back together. By this time, Michael was a self-assured businessman and would only get back together if he had complete control of the group. He let Davie pick the name, figuring how much harm could that cause. Since that time, Davie has been the star but Michael has been the stabilizer.

One of my previous positions at the bank was in the loan office. I had the unenviable assignment of calling those who were in arrears on their payments and informing them of our foreclosure policy. Over a ten-year period, the bank repossessed Davie's house, truck, and a couple of cars. We repossessed everything except his twang record. I'll tell you this though, Davie was always respectful through all of his tribulations; unlike some of his wives who used plenty of foreign sounding language. Sometimes he was very philosophical about the foreclosures, saying it all fit into a larger plan. It seemed at the time that his logic was full of holes or fostered by dope.

Then seven years ago, Davie stopped into the bank and started chatting me up. I knew he was still pretty dependent on drugs and wondered what he was thinking. Did he imagine that I had his repossessed vehicles parked in my back yard? Then a few days later he called me up and asked for a date. That call sure caused an explosion to scatter my emotions. I remembered those raging passions I had the first time I saw him perform. Then those agonizing foreclosure phone calls and meetings at the bank. Also, I seriously wondered why he had dumped four wives. We finally made a deal. It was the bravest thing I had ever attempted. If he would go into rehabilitation, dry out and open a savings account at the bank, we would try a date. Davie checked himself into the no fun, no frills Brown County Mental Health and took the cure. After that he moved in with Michael and his family for a couple of months. Michael had three teenagers at the time. Davie would complain to me that it was like prison with hot and cold running teenagers. He opened a savings account at the bank, thus clearing the way for us to start dating. A few months later he moved in with me. Green Bay is small enough that everybody knows everybody else's business. Oh boy did that have the tongues a wagging from Schammico to De Pere. That was six wonderful years ago. And the rest is history. Ha, I've always wanted to say that.

    That was good; no juicy stuff so far. I still can't believe that the woman who used to be the shyest girl in Green Bay is going to tell you this story. You could say our adventure started about a year ago.

Chapter Two
October 16, 1997
Green Bay, Wisconsin

Over the previous few weeks, Roy had been having the boys perform on Thursday night as well as the weekend. That Thursday Davie went to Roy's right after supper and I did a few loads of laundry. Being a working girl I took a little nap before going down to The Dog.

When I walked into The Howling Dog, The Word was singing out a saucy Southern song *I Like It I Love It Can't Get Enough Of It*. Roy Ryman, bartender extraordinaire, was swabbing the bar and swaying to that toe tapping Tim McGraw music. Roy always had my stool saved at the end of the bar no matter how busy they were. If some foreigner tried to sit on my reserved perch, Roy would launch into his hyperbolic explanation about why the stool needed to be kept open. The stranger would usually leave with a dazed look and warn his friends about the consequences of sitting in that particular place.

If you looked around the bar, you knew it was a direct reflection of the owner's personality. Here's what one local newspaper had to say about the place. "Sitting in the heart of down trodden down town Green Bay, in an old gray stone turned black stone, is The Howling Dog Saloon. One must not be misled by the understated exterior, as the interior is an abundance of beer and country potpourri. Every available surface supports all manner of beer signs, including the Hamm's dancing bears, the bold black Potosi logo, and Big Chief himself. The owner, Mr. Roy Ryman, never met a promotion he didn't fully ingest. Posters of country music stars abound, covering every inch of The Dog. From the pretty Miss Kitty to Trish and Tammy. There are large glossies of Merle and Reba, flanked by Lyle and Loretta. And in one corner, life sized posters of John and June. A string of chili pepper lights encircles the room, creating a musty metaphor for the smell of stale saloon. Left over from the Tangerine A-Go-Go are mismatched tables and duct-taped chairs. All in all, The Howling Dog provides a homey, comfy atmosphere for the denizens of De Pere and the lost souls of Ashwaubenon." That's what one local writer said, and unfortunately, I couldn't have captured it better.

After being there about twenty minutes one of the regulars started calling out for me to do a song. It has been very interesting becoming part of this saloon scene. Some of my friends there were the ones that started calling me banker chick. Kind of a weird nickname, but the only one I've ever had. I was too much of a loner in the past for anyone to care about giving me a nickname. Makes me feel very accepted. Over the years with Davie, we had worked up a couple of songs that I performed. Don't think for a minute that it was easy going from being so shy to performing with Michael and Davie. At first I would get on and off of the stage as fast as possible. We spent many long nights at the apartment with Davie coaching his heart out. He started out giving me small parts and letting me harmonize along with him. It grew from there. That night I did a Mary Chapin Carpenter song that was one of my favorites. *I Feel Lucky* really turned me loose. No longer that serious banker chick, I mentally disconnected and became a bar room beaut. Most exhilarating. The patrons gave me hearty applause and a couple of catcalls as I returned to my stool.

Shortly after I finished the crowd began thinning out and it was creeping up on closing time.

"I'm ready for some serious strategizing and confabulating," Roy told me. He meant the after hours chat sessions between him and the boys.

My Davie stepped to the microphone, twelve-gallon hat looming on his head and said, "We want to do a little piece for you that is one of my favorites." With his charismatic smile, he waved the bow and fiddle in the air, and stomped out the count.

"Early on one beautiful morn,
Fiddled as soon as I was born.
Sitting on my mommy's knee
Counting the rhythm, one, two, three.

I was the coolest teen around,
The bestest fiddler in Bay town.
Sitting on the groupie's knee,
Kissing 'em all, one, two, three.

Up on stage with my friend Maki
Fiddling 'round, feeling wacky
Sitting on the owner's knee,
Counting dollars, one, two, three.

Living is fun if you fiddle
Life ain't nothing but a holey holy riddle."

Bouncing off of the baubles and beer displays, the last few strays gave Michael and Davie scattered applause.

"Do you have any requests," Davie asked as the last lost souls veered out The Dog's door. "Are there more requests?" asked a deadpan Davie, as Roy stretched across the bar as far as he could. With his fingertips, Roy pulled the plug out of the wall causing the amps to squeak and go dead.

"You Bulls can stop bellarin," Roy began. "Just save that Bovine Growth Hormone for the weekend. You know come the weekend, this is the place to squeal with the veal. I may even run a promotion for the heifer that comes dressed looking the most like Elsie," he finished looking very pleased with himself and his quotations from the Book of Roy.

Davie came over to the bar, gave me a hug and took off his twelve-gallon hat, freeing his salt and pepper ponytail that had been hidden under the hat. The boys took their usual after hour's places, and Davie turned his hat upside down on the bar. For years the boys had worn regular ten-gallon hats. Then Al Framp over at Triple D Western Wear got a shipment of these twelve-gallon hats that weren't moving. He called Michael and tried to give him two twelve-gallon hats for advertisement. Michael stopped at the Triple D one day, tried out the hats and talked a deal. Now on a burly lunker like Michael a twelve-gallon looks pretty good. But on an average guy like Davie, it makes him look more like a caricature. On the other hand, they were each getting a hundred dollars a year from Framp just to wear his hats.

"An Elsie contest?" asked Davie in mock horror as he reached into his hat and pulled out a bag of home grown tobacci. "Roy, the secret to life is purity. How could you despoil the purity of this orchestral sanctuary with another adulterated promotion?"

Michael saw the opening he wanted. "Roy, if you want us fresh for the weekend. You can stuff this Thursday night bop in the woodshed," he said, while trying to give Roy his professional glare. "I'm not twenty-four any more. I have a real life, with a business, and a family. Making you rich is just my hobby."

Davie nodded some kind of agreement. I'm not sure if he was supporting Michael or congratulating himself on having rolled a perfect joint of Maui Wowie.

"We need you to entertain the onslaught of Packer fans," said Roy.

"It's not my fault they won the Super Bowl," replied Michael.

"Michael, it's called opportunity."

"It's as hectic as heavy metal at the music store. We're already deep into Christmas. And every Suzuki mom wants her kid to be the next Davie Fender."

"Imagine, tumultuous times at the tune store," offered Roy.

"I'm also working on the summer schedule for country star and myself."

"Do you mean that you are running off again next summer and leaving me looking for entertainers down at the knackers. Do you know, that last summer some couple traveled all the way from La Crosse to listen to you two. And you were at the Minnesota State Fair."

"We have now heard that story eighteen times. It looks like we'll be at both the Minnesota and Wisconsin State Fairs next summer."

Up until then Davie had just been listening. That was usually his style. He was such a stepper on stage, but otherwise he was a pretty mellow fellow, who enjoyed listening and reflecting. That probably explains how he wrote *Wallowing Wuv*. I think that he got started with drugs, because they augmented his on stage persona. "You don't need to book a lot of out of towners for me," Davie said.

"Did you hear that?" asked Roy. "Davie is satisfied here with all of his sins in a row. He's got his substance sins, simmering sins, situational sins, succulent sins, smoldering sins, and simulated sins."

"We have to travel. We're advertising and building our fan base. I've contacted the Hodag Festival in Rhinelander, and Fan Fare in Nashville."

"Maki, you know they aren't going to invite us back to Fan Fare," said Davie.

An incident many years ago, when Davie was doing lots of pot and pills, gained The Word a questionable reputation with Fan Fare. Their performances were creating some swell reviews, but then things got pretty sticky when their friend Loretta invited them to the Crisco Booth. Davie started signing autographs with Crisco. First, a couple of little cookies got upset because he got Crisco on their new shirts and jackets. Then he started signing body parts. Every little cupcake wanted a more adventurous autograph than the one before her. A couple hundred fans stormed the booth. First it was just the tipsy masses clawing and shoving for a better view. In a few minutes the real maniacs arrived shouting for more. Then the perverts showed up clutching whatever they could. Sheer pandemonium. To hear Davie tell the story, it all ended with two hundred frenzied bodies in one mammoth pile. And they haven't been invited back since.

"They can't remember the Crisco Kid forever," Michael said.

"Did you ever write that song, *I Left My Heart in Star Fans Crisco?*" asked Roy.

"I don't care what you two say. We are traveling," stated Michael.

"My crowds are at least twice as big when you gentlemen are here," Roy continued, noting that he was dimming Michael's professional glow with time and words.

"They are bigger because we travel. You should pay us to travel." Said Michael, hoping that the mention of more money would get Roy's attention.

"Last year I ended up with Gus, the one armed accordion player."

"And the really sad part is that Gus didn't sit here until 3:00 AM listening to you and your confabulations," said Michael.

"I lose money every time you strays travel."

"Roy, you are starting to irritate me," said the usually unflappable Michael.

"I'd just as soon not travel this summer," said Davie as he inhaled deeply.

My Marlboro man really had not been feeling well. Over the last two years he had been slowing down. At first I felt it was my fault. But it was Davie.

Roy was becoming insistent and hadn't heard Davie. "I may have another house band when you prodigal sons return."

"Where's the love?" asked Davie, as he exhaled a rich golden plume.

"Do you know how often the owner of the Grizzly Rose calls me? And do you know what he wants? He wants the country star and myself to be his house band," said Michael.

This was not the usual course for our happy go lucky blab sessions. "Wait a minute," I said. "Roy, you know you're not getting another house band. And Michael, you know you're not going to The Grizzly."

"Maybe I would," replied Roy.

"Thanks Marion." said Michael. "I also heard from *Austin City Limits*. They want us to appear at South By South West. They'll send an assistant to evaluate us."

"Michael, even I know that means thanks but no thanks," said Davie.

"We're the top country band in the state, and you have that Dairylang Twang."

"Television doesn't want a duo from Wisconsin playing regressive country music," said Davie.

"We have three hit records."

"Three releases would be more like it," said Davie

"Were those 45s or 78s?" asked Roy, as he hummed, "The Crisco Kid is a pal of mine."

"I'm too tired to travel," said Davie as he exhaled smoke rings toward a penguin on one of Roy's upscale ashtrays.

Chapter Three
September 3, 1997
Rome, Italy

The faded red Fiat 500 sped into the imposing St. Peter's Square, surrounded by hundreds of Carrara marble columns. That racing rosy blur paid little attention to the Berini Porticoes as it whizzed past the expensive sheet metal, rows of tour busses, and pigeons, then flipped into a reserved parking place in front of the Vatican City's Apostolic Palace. A hearty Celt bounced from his toaster oven sized transport and trotted up the marble stairs. His casual dress contrasted to the marble statues and high arching splendor of Vatican City. Straight through the door he proceeded. Paying no attention to the ornate floor to ceiling frescoes, he made his way directly to the receptionist's desk which was manned by a long faced, forward tilting gent, who was squinting through his glasses and wearing a priest's collar.

"I'm Bishop O'Connor. I was told the Pope called for me."

"I'm Father Mostaccioli, the Pope's Outer Secretary. Tell me Bishop, you do play golf, don't you?"

"Yes, I would say I play, after a fashion."

"Very good, we need a golfer. We have a foursome going out this afternoon. How is your health?"

"I'm in excellent health. I'm the youngest Bishop in Ireland."

"Wonderful, truly wonderful."

"I've been studying at The Vatican for a year and this is the first time that the Pope has wanted me to golf with him."

"This is what you would call an urgent situation. And it's not exactly the Pope that is golfing."

"Whom will I be golfing with?"

"The Pope has directed an advisory group of Cardinals to hit the links this afternoon."

"And they were one short?" asked Bishop O'Connor.

"Pray tell me, one short of what?" countered the Outer Secretary in his uniquely oblique style.

"One short of a foursome."

"I don't see it that way. Let me call them and inform them that their expectant has arrived. Bishop, I want to thank you on part of the Holy See for abandoning your studies this afternoon and assisting His Holiness."

"My obligation in life is to follow the will of God."

"Amen Bishop. Please wait while I let them know you are here."

Father Mostaccioli picked up the phone and announced that Bishop O'Connor had arrived. In a matter of seconds the easy going Bishop found himself surrounded by four chattering Cardinals, all wearing miles of red robes, each more eager than the other to welcome him in joining them on the golf course.

This had to be the senior club of Cardinals, Bishop O'Connor surmised to himself. It shouldn't be too hard to score the low round, he thought. I'm generously guessing an average age of seventy-five.

"Bishop, I'm Cardinal Ouie Ouie from Nigeria," said the cheery white haired pontiff, as the Bishop genuflected and kissed the Cardinal's ring. "Were you ever a member of the Irish Republican Army?" asked Ouie Ouie.

The next to greet the Bishop was a frail octogenarian from India. "Bishop, I'm Cardinal Tansi from Bombay. I'm really looking forward to a golf course without water buffalo wandering everywhere."

As Bishop O'Connor started to genuflect the olive skinned Cardinal stopped him. "No Bishop, that's not necessary. We're golfing buddies this afternoon. Like they say, 'We're just wild and crazy guys," said the Indian Cardinal.

"G'day mate, I'm Cardinal Grainger, from Melbourne," said the bronze bonton from behind his pink John Lennon glasses. He gave Bishop O'Connor a quick gesture commensurate with his relaxed style indicating that kissing his ring was not necessary.

"Cardinal, I recognize you," beamed the Irish Bishop. "I've seen you on the telly at the annual blessing of the kangaroos."

"Bonzer Bishop. One of the truly noble things I do. Giving God's glory to all of his creatures."

"Bishop, I'm Cardinal Westwood from the United States. Actually it's unfair, because I pulled your rap sheet and know all about you. While you know very little about us. We like it that way."

Bishop O'Connor extended his hand with the intention of shaking hands with the ruddy American.

"Bishop, you can just kiss my ring."

Cardinal Jim Westwood was a West Texas boy of the Depression, whose family sustained a modest existence during those difficult times on his father's salary as a Shinola salesman. Young Jim listened to the far off radio signals of Houston and Dallas trying desperately to hear the latest Sons of The Pioneer's recording. He daydreamed of having his own band and touring the country. Those dreams began to fade when he was excused from the church choir in fourth grade. Another blow to his plans occurred at the Davey Crocket Middle School, where he was locked out of the music room. His fantasy finally evaporated when he was banned from the local music store for his inability to listen to the demo records without making them warp. Wanting to guarantee himself a college education, he enrolled in a Franciscan Seminary. He rapidly reached the rank of cardinal by outliving his contemporaries.

"You have a foursome. Why do you need me?" asked Bishop O'Connor.

"The Pope told us to play some golf and do some brainstorming for his next world tour. And none of us golf," explained the always pleasant Cardinal Ouie Ouie of Africa.

Greener than the land of shamrocks, the rolling hills of the Vatican Golf Course had been cleared of all other golfers. Lush links and tall Chestnut trees formed nature's own chapel.

More pure and piney than a thousand spritzes of a Glade air freshener, the course welcomed the five some and their Swiss Guards. Looking more splendid than peacocks, the first cart of two Swiss Guards took great delight in leading the parade and setting the pace. Next in this waggish procession were two concerned looking cardinals bouncing and straining to keep up. Riding by himself in the third cart was the perplexed Bishop O'Connor. Hurrying to keep up were two more cardinals in the fourth cart followed by two more speeding peacocks.

After a punishing ten-minute ride that seemed way longer; all of the Cardinals were relieved to have arrived without incident. The Vatican guardsmen immediately swarmed around the Cardinals, and ignored the Bishop, leaving him to struggle with his golf bag. Cardinal Westwood broke ranks and approached the Bishop.

"I don't usually play golf, but I have to tell you the greens on this course are very fast," said the American Cardinal.

By this time the golfing Celt was the eye of a target with a ring of Cardinals around him and a ring of guards around them. "How do you know that?" he replied.

"Last week Archbishop Nelson told me in confession that he had used profanity on this course because of the fast greens," Westwood answered.

"Who is Archbishop Nelson?" asked the Bishop.

"He's the Archbishop from Texas," answered Cardinal Westwood.

"Big man, big divots," added the diminutive Cardinal Tansi of India.

"Nelson too loud to be Cardinal," offered the soft-spoken Cardinal from Africa.

"He's no friend to Kangaroos. Once he boxed a kangaroo and knocked it out," added the Cardinal who was the friend of kangaroos everywhere. "He needs a bloody good penance."

"Bishop please kneel a minute," requested the kindly Cardinal Ouie Ouie. "I will bless you and your golf implements there. I want you to score the highest score in the whole world, what ever that would be. I also pray you don't kill someone with a wild shot. Amen."

"Amen," repeated the Bishop as he surveyed the completely vacated course.

"Wait ohhmm, a minute," hummed Cardinal Tansi of India. He put his hands over the Bishop's folded hands and directed him, "Please close your eyes and breathe deeply. Breathe deeply and let all of the bad shots escape from your body. Breathe. Concentrate on the good golf karma flowing into your body." He paused briefly. "Amen."

"We don't have good golf karma in the Catholic Church," stated Cardinal Westwood.

"I'm from India and we have good karma for everything, even Cardinals wandering in tall poppies."

The Bishop's eyes darted nervously toward the one Cardinal who had volunteered nothing so far.

"I'll give you a free pass on this hole," said the Australian, Cardinal Grainger peering at the Bishop over the top of his glasses. What club are you going to use?"

"I think I can get on the green with a three iron."

"The Trinity," added Cardinal Tansi.

Hesitantly Bishop O'Connor approached the first tee and took some practice swings. With a continuous chorus of ohhhs and ahhhs behind him he placed the ball on the tee.

"Would anyone like to make a little gentlemanly wager on his score?" asked the Cardinal from down under.

"I worry that the Pope is getting to old to travel," belted out Cardinal Westwood ignoring the wager remark.

"Now, now, he told me that if Mick Jagger could continue touring, he could continue touring," answered Cardinal Ouie Ouie.

Whack. The Bishop had hit a sizzling slice half way to the green and deep into the rough. Almost in unison he heard the voices behind him.

"Oh God, forgive him."

"Out of bounds."

"That's a sticky wicket."

"Next time I'd use the six. If you can get half way with the three, you could get all the way with the six."

Does Tiger Woods have pressure like this the Bishop asked himself?

Bishop O'Connor got into his cart and went in search of his shank shot. The Cardinals appraised their ruby robes versus the deep rough, and continued to cluster on the first tee to discuss the next world tour.

Cardinal Westwood began again, "Naturally the Pope should come to the U.S. You know how he likes Roy Rogers and the old west."

"With all due respect Cardinal, the last time I visited you in America you promised me that we'd meet Willie Nelson. It never happened. I thought His Holiness's world tour should have a spiritual theme," said Cardinal Tansi. "The good Mother Theresa just passed, I know His Excellency would like to visit India and pay tribute to her."

"Yes, and then swing by for a stop at the Sydney Opera House," added Cardinal Grainger.

"I'm sure I can get all of you an audience with Emmy Lou Harris," said the American Cardinal.

"Wait, we need to organize this discussion," said Cardinal Ouie Ouie.

"Wait! Bishop O'Connor is getting away," said the Australian Cardinal.

Bishop O'Connor had skipped the second tee and headed on to the third tee, thinking that perhaps he could finish his round of golf without further blessings. Instead he triggered a Chinese Fire Drill. The Vatican guards and the Cardinals scrambled for their golf carts and headed off, bobbing up and down over the turf until they caught the Bishop.

"Pray, tell us how is it going?" inquired the tenderhearted Cardinal Ouie Ouie.

"I've had worse rounds," replied the Bishop. "Although I'm not sure when."

"Maybe this is the time for me to give you the blessing that I give the kangaroos," added Cardinal Grainger. "May you hop the links and hit the holes with all of your Joeys safely in tow. Amen. A friendly wager anyone?"

The Bishop sprinted away from the Cardinals, quickly teed up the ball, grabbed his club, and swung. Blap, he hit a little blooper barely fifty feet down the fairway.

"May God forgive him."

"Amen. Let's organize our discussion," said the Cardinal from Africa as he tried once again. "Let's each take a turn and tell what he thinks the goals of the Pope's trip should be. I'll listen to your ideas and go last."

"I think that the trip should show that Catholics are reaching out to animals. It would be apropos for the Pope to travel to the Outback and attend the blessing of the kangaroos," said Cardinal Grainger in all earnestness as he peered over his spectacles.

"I believe that the Pope should be the messenger of hope," started Cardinal Tansi. His mere presence inspires people. In India we have the most wide spread poverty of any country in the world, we just lost our spiritual soul, Mother Theresa. Without a doubt he should come to India."

"Appealing to animals is good," began Cardinal Westwood, "but they don't contribute very much, if you know what I mean. And hope is good. But I was thinking of a larger goal. My vision is that The Church align itself with country western music."

"You know, I met Rick Springfield one time," added the Aussie Cardinal.

"Thank you," said Cardinal Ouie Ouie, ever the peacemaker. "I believe that His Excellency should have two goals. His goodness should be a support to struggling people through out the world. As you know, South Africa is emerging from years of Apartheid. If the Pope would visit South Africa it would give them a world stage and added support for their new government. Secondly, the Pope should use his visit to honor good Catholics, like Father Cypria of Nigeria, who has performed numerous miracles."

"If we don't use divine intervention with the music industry we're going to get more songs like *Butterfly Kisses*," implored the American Cardinal.

"The Pope could attend the Festival of Lights in New Delhi," said the Indian Cardinal, losing hope for his original suggestion.

"With all due respect dear gentlemen Cardinals, we have some very different ideas. How can we reconcile them?" asked Cardinal Ouie Ouie.

"We can combine them," added the ever-mystical Cardinal of the kangaroos. "His Excellency could attend the Festival of Lights, accompanied by an impoverished kangaroo, while singing a country western song."

"No!" replied Cardinal Tansi. Let's find a totally impartial way to resolve this."

At that moment the opportunistic American Cardinal had an idea that was bound to make his day. Beaming like an angel in harpsichord heaven, Cardinal Westwood explained, "Now Cardinal Grainger you're a sporting man and would enjoy a little wager." He then draped his arm around the diminutive Cardinal Tansi; "I know how we can guarantee impartiality." He gave Cardinal Ouie Ouie his best Cheshire smile. "As always Cardinal, we lean on you to get us organized. I have a plan that will satisfy all of you. We'll let the Bishop's score decide whose plan we recommend to the Pope. Now a good golfer would score between seventy and eighty on this course. We know that isn't going to happen. Cardinal Grainger I'll give you every score of ninety or below. Cardinal Tansi I'll give you ninety-one to one hundred. Cardinal Ouie Ouie I'll give you any score from one hundred one to one hundred ten. It would be impossible to score higher than that, but I'll take one hundred eleven and higher. If the Bishop gets your score, we recommend your plan."

"I would say his game is in God's hands and only God's hands," added Bishop Tansi, fearing it was already in Westwood's pocket.

The Bishop was almost out of sight. "Stop him," yelled Cardinal Westwood, "he needs one more good blessing."

The party recarted and the chase was on. Bishop O'Connor was captured on the sixth tee. With a vortex of crimson cardinals and rainbow guards swirling around him, the Bishop was reblessed. He continued the final holes with all of the Cardinals talking, repeatedly making the sign of the cross, and telling Irish jokes. His final score was one hundred forty, give or take five strokes. Supporting South Africa, providing hope to India, and blessing the kangaroos would have to wait; the advisory group of Cardinals had weighed in with their decision. The Catholic Church was headed in a bold new direction. Country Music.

Cardinal Westwood's temporary Vatican residence was a luxurious suite on the third floor of the Apostolic Palace. That evening, after dining on succulent roast duck and sipping sage Marsala wine, the Cardinal started planning his bold aspirations for His Excellency's next world tour. He drifted off to sleep with visions of Willie, Waylon, and the Pope.

The Next Morning

Cardinal Westwood picked up the pearl Victorian phone on his carved Sicilian desk and punched in twenty digits. He then waited for the voice on the other end of the phone.

"Who the hell is calling me at 3:00AM?" demanded Archbishop Nelson.

"This is Cardinal Westwood, and I've called to talk to you about your profanity."

"I was asleep. What in God's name do you want?"

"I've figured out your penance for using irreligious language on the Vatican golf course."

"Good night and go to… Just go to bed," said the Archbishop as he slammed down the phone.

Chapter Four
October 22, 1997
Green Bay, Wisconsin

Did you ever try to get a musician up in the morning? Those creatures of the night don't want to move in the morning. That's the way it was when I first took Davie to the doctor. Months of nagging, plus some severe abdominal pain had finally paid off.

In every department it was the same questions, "Are you Mrs. Fender?"

"No."

"Are you his daughter?"

"No!"

"How are you related?"

"By circumstances."

Someone once suggested we were partners. Now that notion really warms me up. Not. Well, maybe we're partners in the helpful sense. But I've seen too many detached creepy business partners to like that term.

In some departments of the Bellengood Clinic I could go with him, and in other areas I was asked to make like a mushroom in their waiting room. That gave me way too much time for thinking. Like that year when the boys were playing at the Wisconsin State Fair's Pabst Pavilion. It was a five-day stint, the pay was substantial and the benefits were good, especially if you like Pabst beer. On the third day Davie came up missing and Michael had to search the three square miles of grounds to find him. Finally, two days later Michael found him totally stoned in the cow barn officiating a milking contest. They got a two-year suspension from the fair for that one.

Another incident occurred after The Word had just spent a week performing at The Hodag Festival in Rhinelander and Davie had returned full of awe. He was enthralled by the beautiful music and the gorgeous north piney woods. *The Kentucky Waltz, The Tennessee Waltz, and Waltzing Matilda* had inspired him to start creating that mellow yet peppy ditty, *The Rhinelanderer Philanderer.* However, he was with wife number three, they were strung out all of the time, and therefore it was never completed. It is absolutely unthinkable to throw away those rhyming possibilities: pander, slander, and one night stander. I know it would have been every bit as big as *Brown Eyed Handsome Cow.*

Those things happened when he was with his four wives. It's hard to admit that the man you love squandered a ton of talent. I sure wish that I could turn back the clock. Maybe I could have kept him safe. Well, maybe. Who am I kidding? Davie wouldn't have given me a tumble in high school. He dated all of those sexy cheerleaders. We were from different planets all right, Mercury and Pluto.

The girls at the bank used to gossip about Davie; naturally that was before he and I became an item. They would say stuff like, "that Davie Fender's dad was so rich and he had such good schooling. How can he act so dumb?" Mostly they blamed his parents. Myself, I think it was opportunity. Otto's money gave Davie the opportunity to excel at some things and to fail at others. He grew up with a never-ending safety net.

Not like I didn't have enough on my mind, thinking about Davie and his abdominal pains, going to departments where one can barely pronounce the names, and making like a mushroom. Dino Bina was a doctor in that very clinic. Remember Dino, the puny non-native that I smacked in the kisser. After that incident he developed some kind of a nervous condition, became a real bookworm and went into pre-med after high school. Just think, I caused him to develop a personality complex, and now he's a psychiatrist here at Bellengood. Sitting in those waiting rooms, I worried that Dr. Dino would tap me on the shoulder and ask in his unmistakably tamed down tone, "is that you Marion?" That was enough thinking about stuff.

Reading is another one of my hobbies. Actually, the way I see it, understanding life isn't just for the Dahlia Lama and those skinny guys in white robes. Anyway, I wanted to know the meaning of life for a tall, devoted, small town girl, and not short men living in caves. Out of all of the clinic's magazines, I found one called Chromosomes Are Fun, which had an article titled Life Is a DNA Riddle. Now telling you all of this is pretty embarrassing, but here goes. Reproductive

Scientists are working on a technique called Selective Chromosome Alignment, which is designed to make every baby the utmost expression of the positive traits of the parents. At the time of conception, this technique facilitates the noblest chromosomes of the father combining with the elite eggs of the mother to create a superlative reflection of the parents. The article left me thinking about my weathered, leathered hombre. He was a musician like his mother. They both had the same eyes that illuminated their ephemeral soul. On stage he was dazzling, which was something Helen never wanted to try. But Davie was definitely not the businessman his father was. He did have his father's perseverance, which probably explains the four marriages. Davie got his chromosomes the old-fashioned way, which turned into severe disappointment for his father. And what if he had turned out to be the conservative owner of Fender Ford. We would have never met. Well, I wanted to ponder that another day. Five hours and seven departments was definitely a mind-numbing day. I was exhausted and ready to go home. We had to wait a week for all of the lab results and another visit, but you didn't need to be Dr. Laura to see all of their concerned expressions.

    When Davie decided to detour through The Dog on our way home, I knew he was feeling some serious tension. We arrived through an unlocked door without the hint of a human anywhere. Davie yelled into the backroom and called down to the basement but Roy was not around. My man poured himself a Special Export and made me a Shirley Temple. He took my hand, held it tightly, and told me how much he cared for me. "I need you more than Hank Jr. needs *Monday Night Football*," he said as he snuggled up really close to me. I told him Roy might return at any minute. He said that frankly he didn't give a damn, as he put his arm around my shoulder and heartily pulled me toward him. Actually, that's all I can tell you about our visit to the clinic.

Chapter Five
October 25, 1997
Green Bay, Wisconsin

"Yes, Life's just one big Saturday night," shouted Davie, as he threw his outstretched arms into the air. "Thank you. We are The Word, the last word in country music. I especially want to thank all of you fine bovine women that took part in the Elsie contest here tonight. I had no idea there were so many Elsie fans around Green Bay. We have one final tune for you this evening." He grinned and stomped.

"Never do worry 'bout my luck,
I just bought a used pick up truck.
Sitting on the dealer's knee,
Counting cylinders, one, two, three.

After Davie they broke the mold.
All the rest, they've got the gold.
Sitting on my banker's knee,
Counting the debits, one, two, three.

Maki and me playing the dives,
Trying hard to pay my wives.
Sitting on my therapists knee,
Counting divorces one, two, three.

Living is fun if you fiddle.
Life ain't nothing but a holey holy riddle."

"You all have a good trip home. Drive safely, and pray for me."

Davie grabbed hold of the electrical plug before winsome Roy could and then gave him a corny stare, as the last dogged patrons gave the boys an appreciative ovation. "You're the man, Davie. You're the man."

Now I had probably sat in on a thousand of these sessions and that was the first time I ever heard Davie say pray for me.

"You were stallions out there tonight," bantered Roy in plagiarized pontification. "Blazing Saddles. You were more nimble than polo ponies. I had visions of Affirmed, Secretariat, and Julie Krone running wild. It was like the reincarnation of Black Beauty, Trigger, and Mr. Ed. You thoroughbreds deserve more hay tonight," he concluded, as we took up our usual spots at the end of the bar.

"Does that translate into more money?" asked Michael, already knowing the answer.

"Not exactly."

"So, did you boys kiss and make up?" I asked, wanting to make sure the hard feelings of last Thursday night were completely put to rest.

"Roy can't stay mad very long. He's afraid of being here alone at 3:00 AM and talking to himself," said Michael, as the reflection of the Hamm's Bears danced against his glass.

"I ain't kissin no one. But everything's cool with me and the music man," boasted Roy more for show than anything else.

"What was that remark about pray for me?" asked Michael

"Marion and I are thinking about going back to church," replied Davie.

"I thought that the Catholic Church wouldn't give you your fourth annulment," said Roy.

"They said I wasn't sincere enough for another annulment."

"Maybe you weren't rich enough for another annulment," Roy countered. "Davie, you need to smoke a little dope. You're good at faking sincerity after a joint or two."

"I've applied about a dozen times, stoned and sober."

"So how are you going to attend mass?" Roy persisted.

"There's always the Saturday afternoon mass."

"Ya, I guess the requirements are bloomin' loose at that mass," said Roy. "So, do you believe in angels?" asked Roy.

"Of course I believe in angels. If I didn't have a guardian angel, I probably would have perished in one of my many misadventures."

"Misadventures!" Roy proclaimed. "Technically, you should be in jail."

"First it's pray for me, now it's guardian angels. I thought I knew you," quizzed Michael.

"Sure, I've got a little stubby legged guardian angel. He's so short because I've run his little legs into the ground," said Davie.

I'd heard Davie ruminating about that stubby legged guardian angel before, but I think this was the first time he had sprung it on the after hours party. The look on Roy's face was priceless.

"Do you think that the Pope is infallible?" asked Michael.

"Of course he inhales," answered Davie. "If he walked in right now I'd offer him a reefer."

"That was either a bad joke or blasphemy," said Michael.

"Either way it was a sin," said Roy. "Do you think that priests should marry?"

"Definitely," Davie responded. "Anybody can get to heaven if they are single."

"Do you believe that children are a gift from God? asked Roy.

"It depends if you believe that God is a loving God or a vengeful God," Davie replied.

"Roy, are you going to put up a Christmas tree this year?" I asked as I debated what to tell Roy and Michael about Davie's situation. I knew Davie wouldn't say a word about nothing. He'd have to be in the hospital in a coma before he would admit anything, especially to these two.

"Last year some cowboy started my tree on fire and we had to douse it with beer," Roy answered.

"I think you started the fire just to sell more beer," Michael added.

"Well, between the beer sales and the insurance claim, it was a fairly good fire."

Finally I had the confidence and the words that I wanted. I told the boys that Davie had been in to the Bellengood Clinic for a series of tests. Naturally, Roy and Michael didn't take it very seriously.

"Did you stay up all night studying?" asked Roy, trying to resurrect a seriously wounded high school joke.

"Sounds like an ulcer to me." said Michael who had, according to himself, never been sick a day in his life, and couldn't understand illness in others.

"We know how stressful it is having Marion wait on you 24/7," said Roy, with just a hint of jealousy.

"He has to be fine," said Michael. "Next week, I'm calling *Austin City Limits* and talking to Larry Tacoma personally. He doesn't realize it yet but we're just the group he's looking for."

Chapter Six
October 28, 1997
Austin, Texas

Worlds away from wanton Wisconsin during the psychedelic seventies country music was evolving. It flourished like weed in Music City, USA. As honky tonk met gospel, Nashville was enjoying enormous prosperity. Country fans wanted the latest Charlie Pride and Crystal Gale records to play on their ole Victrolas. Times were so good that the Gibson guitar was being replaced by the Wall Street Journal as the instrument of choice. The establishment became more interested in the bottom line than the banjo line. Diversity and creativity suffered. Sounds of suffering lead to licks of frustration, thus breeding chords of discontent, and causing bands of revolution. Two young Texas troubadours blew out of the hills just north of the Alamo to lead this revolution. Soon the swirl of outlaw country music engulfed all of central Texas. The epicenter of this airwave was Austin's Texas Turkey Cafe. As the crescendo grew it reached the most unlikely of places, KLRU, Public Broadcasting, Austin, Texas.

Experiencing an ever-growing lament as one after another of his easy listening stations changed to a country format Sig Eros, KLRU Executive Director, began to think that there was something to this country music phenomenon. One morning after nightmares about the state of public television, Sig awoke to find he had split open his pillow and had a mouth full of turkey feathers. Already feeling down in the mouth, Sig's thoughts turned to the Texas Turkey Cafe. Maybe it was a sign from God. That night he tasted of the foreboding fiddle licks and liked it.

Sig, a Black Angus of a man who was as keen and crafty as an Edward G. Robinson character, suggested that their station host a country music show, which caused great internal discord. The debate raged on with some saying that public broadcasting was not meant to be popular, but painful. KLRU's Station Manager Porter, some months the only cloud in South Texas, joined the debate and probed for the educational merits of country music. In the end intellectual debate lost out to manipulation and connivance and in 1976 *Austin City Limits* was born. Thousands of citizens were heard to exclaim: "my god maw can you believe some hotsy totsy hit parade being on that educational channel."

Sig's right hand man was the Twiggiesque Program Director, Larry Tacoma. All hair and brains. His fervent nature allowed him to overlook the pervasive poverty of public broadcasting and produce a divine product. Larry's cat like quickness had kept him one step ahead of Porter. Together he and Sig were the oil and vinegar who had created that tangy Texas treat.

Sig and Larry shared a large room that they hesitantly called an office. It had all of the clutter and none of the charm of *Sanford and Son's*. The room was really a twenty-year aggregation of mismatched file cabinets, cluttered bulletin boards and dilapidated old chairs. Sig had a large wooden desk completely lost in piles of paper. Sitting at a forty five-degree angle to Sig's desperate situation was Larry's gray metal desk stacked high with audio and videotapes.

On that particular October day, Larry was expressing his frustration at the large number of groups clamoring to appear on their show. "I've got them all Sig. I've got them from A to Z. We've got to develop a way to wade through all of these tapes and letters. Here's a letter from the Alaskan Athabascan, a harmonica band from somewhere in Nebraska. Over there is something from Zen and The Zydeco Zen Buddhist. They're three guys playing country music on harps. We're drowning in our own success. I need an assistant."

"Porter said you'd get an assistant when Texas freezes over," said Sig. "Have you heard from Wisconsin's number one country band?"

"Oh yes, I've heard from The Word."

"How can you be so down on a group that has appeared at Fan Fare and The Hodag Festival?"

"Fan Fare management won't say much about them. Seems they pulled some kind of slick business with the fans."

"Embezzlement?"

"No. I don't really think they are quick enough for that."

"Did you call Rhinelander?"

"It's one of those Wisconsin towns that's only open during the summer. They've closed up already."

"Where else have they appeared?"

"Their letter says they are udderly renowned at the Wisconsin State Fair."

"If they're the number one country band in Wisconsin, why don't you give them a chance?"

"That's Polka land up there. They're probably the only country band."

"How have their demo tapes sounded?"

"They've got a guy that plays a zinger of a fiddle. And their twang could curdle milk. But I bet you a long horn that Michael Vaughnovich would show up with a tuba. They are the house band at The Growling Hog. That sure sounds like a polka place to me. This is the group that wrote *Wallowing Wuv*."

"Yes that Bill Tillis hit," Sig remembered, as he sang out the refrain, "You were a swine sent from above. Now I'm stuck in Wallowing Wuv."

"Anyway, I've sent them rejection letter A, rejection letter B, and rejection letter C."

"Did you try sending them to South By South West?"

"Yes, that's part of rejection letter C."

"Larry, have you talked to Kris Kristofferson about doing a show?"

"I've talked to his agent who wants me to fly to Nashville."

"To talk to Kris?"

"No, the agent."

"I know Porter will pop for you to fly, when you can catch a ride on the back of an Armadillo."

"I know Kris would do it if I could talk to him directly."

"Well little buddy," said skipper Sig to his Gilligan, "we have bigger problems than that. I talked to Porter yesterday and he turned down our request for new cameras. Furthermore, he said it's going to take three months to get the editing machine fixed. You're going to have to drive to San Antonio and use their equipment."

"It's embarrassing to be poor," said Larry as he played with his nose.

"And damn inconvenient."

"I know how we could raise some money. Governor Bush could sell a couple of counties back to Mexico," said Larry as he ran his fingers through his springy hair.

"Or Ted Turner," said Sig, as he noted Larry's facial play.

"Good idea, I think he's done buying New Mexico," said Larry, making fishy faces with his mouth.

"Well little buddy back to reality. There is no money to improve the phone system. Porter might get us answering machines. He started laughing when I asked about assistants. We are going to have to grab every roadie we can and put them to work as stage hands."

"Roadies as stage hands? I don't think it could get any more difficult. So what's up for this afternoon?"

"Porter wants us to meet with a Bishop."

"I hope he's coming to make a large donation."

****

That afternoon Sig and Larry met in their office minutes before the arrival of the Bishop.

"I found out that we are being visited by Archbishop Nelson, the highest ranking Catholic in the Southwestern United States. Porter told me it's very important and that we should try to cooperate," said Sig.

"There goes my donation idea," said Larry as he twisted his face into a spastic grimace.

"Let's quickly change our office into a conference room," said Sig as he pushed his desk to one side and the stacks of paper slid into each other. He grabbed the phone and set it on a shelf, while Larry pushed his desk to the other side causing several tapes to fall onto the floor. Larry scrambled for the tapes as Sig got a wooden card table out of the closet. The phone began ringing as Sig was setting up the card table.

Larry dumped the tapes onto his desk and asked, "Where did that phone go?"

The persistent phone rang again as Sig was pushing chairs around the card table. "It's over there, just get it."

Ringing for the third time, the phone would not be ignored. "Hello, Larry Tacoma here," he finally answered.

"Oh you're Michael Vaughnovich from Wisconsin. Actually Michael you caught me at kind of a bad time."

There was a knock on the door and their secretary announced, "Archbishop Nelson is here."

"Michael can I put you on hold." Larry reached up and turned on a little radio to low volume. He located the stapler in the mess. "Now I'm going to put you on hold." He clicked the stapler into the phone and laid the receiver next to the radio.

At that moment Archbishop Nelson, all 6' 4" burst into the room. He was definitely a heavy weight in the Catholic Church. Sig looked at the chairs around the table and feared none of them would hold the burly Archbishop. He scurried to get another chair from across the room that he hoped would hold. Larry was dazed. He had just been voice to voice with the persistent Mr. Vaughnovich, and now he was face to face with the largest Catholic he'd ever seen. In all the commotion the telephone receiver fell off the shelf and was dangling behind Sig and Larry. Sig introduced himself and Larry and then offered the Archbishop a seat. Nelson looked suspiciously at the chair then gingerly lowered himself into it. The Archbishop assessed the tottering chair, the jumble of tapes, the dangling receiver, Larry's contorted face, and the tweet tweet of the plastic discordant radio. He had the harrowing feeling that the meeting needed to be hurried along before something unusual happened. He quickly made a large sign of the cross.

"Can I get you some coffee or soda?" asked Sig.

"No, I'm fine," said Archbishop Nelson, as he looked condescendingly at the card table. "We need to end this as soon as possible." He continued, "This is all top secret. I've come here on a very special mission. Next June the Pope is coming to America and wants to appear on your show."

"The Pope is coming to America and wants to appear on our show?" asked an incredulous Sig. "Are you from *Candid Camera*?"

"Yes. No. And I am not a person who jokes!" stated the Archbishop in a stern voice.

Larry's face tightened and his hair straightened.

"We're a country music show," said Sig, trying to remember if he had heard of this sort of confidence scheme on television's *Most Wanted*.

"A country music show. We're a country music show," Larry whined.

Nelson continued, "the Pope is the Dave Thomas of the Catholic Church. He needs to get his message to Americans and the world. Your show really connects with people. You are the number one rated show on educational television."

"We're Public Television, not educational," Sig countered. "I'm sure that one of the major networks would jump at the chance to host the Pope."

"The Pope loves your magnificent outdoor arena. He has told me himself, that is where he wants to say mass for the country."

"Actually," Both Sig and Larry started to speak at the same time. Sig looked at Larry for the first time and noticed his hair was standing straight up.

"Go ahead Larry," said Sig.

"Actually Archbishop, our show is shot in a studio." said Larry as he tried to regroup.

"That's total nonsense young man," said The Archbishop as he stared at Larry. "I've watched your show many times. It's shot in an amphitheater overlooking Austin."

Sig jumped in for the obviously affected Larry. "Honestly, the shows are shot in a studio. We have a very authentic looking background that makes it look like we are outside. We can show you the studio later."

"The Pope is not going to like that."

"June is not good for us," Larry tried again as he wavered on his chair, his hair now completely spiked. "The shows you see in June are taped in the off season when the performers are not on the road."

"What's with you little man?" retorted the resolute Bishop with flashing eyes and raised eyebrows. "I've watched your shows. I know live shows when I see them. The synergy between your audience and the performers. You can't capture that on tape."

"Now look. I mean…, seriously Archbishop, the shows are taped inside a studio and broadcast later. We do not do live television," demanded Sig.

"A-Actually, our performers give us two hours of tape for every hour you see at home," sputtered Larry, his face now wound tighter than a sailor's knot.

"You understand The Pope is going to be here in June and we would have to do it live at that time," demanded the Archbishop, while wondering if Larry was having a seizure.

"W-We don't do live television," said Larry, looking like a southern fried gargoyle.

"We can only do so much," said Sig trying to save Larry and recapture some offense. "He's only the Pope, he's not Ray Charles."

"The Catholic Church and country music have so much in common," said the Archbishop, totally undeterred by Sig's lack of interest and Larry's contortions. "We both see the world as a vale of tears. We see song as redemption," he started with the determination to continue as long as necessary. "We have the Father, the Son and the Holy Ghost. You have Jimmie Rogers, Roy Acuff, and Hank Williams. We have the three wise men. You have Roy Clark. We have the Blessed Virgin. You have Linda Ronstadt. We have Moses wandering in the desert. You have *Hee Haw*. We have the prodigal son. You have Willie Nelson. We have angels. You have Minnie Pearl. We have the crucifixion. You have *Achie Breakie Heart*. We have Rome. You have Nashville. We have Mary Magdalene. You have Dolly Parton. We have Sodom and Gomorra. You have Twitty City and Branson. We have the Garden of Eden. You have *Austin City Limits*." He emphatically thumped on the card table, and paused to take a breath. "When people see the initials J.C. we want them to think of Johnny Cash as well as Jesus Christ."

Sig had set his jaw and firmed his gaze but that thunderous thump was unnerving.

Larry was looking like Noah trapped in the Ark with hundreds of odoriferous animals.

The Archbishop thought to himself, I haven't had this much fun since I was promoting Pagan Babies. He began again; "We've seen your feeble attempts at fund raising. Coffee mugs and tee shirts - how pathetic. You have to sell salvation. Tell them without you it's eternal damnation and twenty four hours daily of *Get Smart*. We want to see country music at every mass. Worldwide exposure. Irish country with bagpipes. Swiss country with alpenhorns. Australian country with a dideridoo. Hula country masses. Globalization. What do you think of that?"

"I think I have to go to the bathroom," whined Larry.

"Not now," Sig commanded.

" I'll send over some rosaries and holy pictures for you."

"That's not necessary. But we're often in need of miracles," said Sig.

"Of course. I can do that. Mr. Eros, I can name a hospital after you. Yes, Eros." He paused. "Eros, maybe I'd better make it a mental health clinic."

Larry was losing all focus and Sig was sensing the inevitable.

The Archbishop stood up, looking like a mountain in front of them. "It's very simple. You can align yourself with the infidels or stand boldly with God. You can act like an atheist or spread the word of God through country music."

Nelson then puffed out his chest, pointed his finger, and gave his most authoritative glare. "Mr. Eros," he started,

"The Pope governs, tells, orders and compels.
He decrees, appoints, presides and anoints.
He canonizes, commands, confers and demands.
He endows, ordains, remands and restrains.
He invests, detects, annuls and directs.
He rules, legislates, announces and manipulates.
He bans, confers, decides and refers.
He sanctifies, inspires, blesses and requires.
He christens, leads, pronounces and precedes.
He baptizes, marries, eulogizes and buries.
He coordinates, authenticates, ordains and excommunicates.
But the Pope does not ask. And most certainly The Pope does not beg." Then he finished with a final gust, "Thank you gentlemen. The Pope will be here Saturday, June 20th. We will be in touch about the details." With that he burst out as he had burst in.

Sig, now a White Angus of a man, noticed the receiver hanging from the shelf. "Why is that phone hanging there?"

"I have no idea," said Larry with both hands holding his face, which now felt like vacuous nutty putty that had melted in the sun. "So did you decide anything?" Larry asked.

"Yes, on June 20th we're saving our souls and losing our audience."

"Oh that."

Chapter Seven
November 5, 1997
Green Bay, Wisconsin

Can you believe Michael called *Austin City Limits* and found out that the Pope was coming? Yes, the big Pope from Rome was coming to Austin. That phone call gave the boys a lot of laughs around Roy's bar. Michael put on his best Texas accent and pleaded, "But it's a country music show, a country music show." Naturally Roy liked the comparison of Johnny Cash to Jesus Christ.

A week later the news wasn't so cheery. Davie was diagnosed with inoperable cancer and his prognosis was poor. That night after he was diagnosed things looked the bleakest. I was driving us home and Davie didn't say a word all the way to the apartment.

Our apartment takes up the entire third floor of what used to be the Charmin Mansion. It has large rooms with high ceilings and ornate woodwork encasement. It was decorated as you might imagine Ken and Barbie's apartment being decorated, provided they had a limited budget and Ken was a very laid back musician. Not to brag, but there was my flair with color and form. I had made a kaleidoscopic collection of over stuffed pillows. We had purchased a sprawling 1940's davenport and had it reupholstered in purple velvet. Pretty hot. Our Jackson Pollock original print that hung on the North wall and changed emphasis as the sun moved through the room was my favorite. And Davie's contribution was the gray guitar cases all over the place. Our coffee table held a collection of music magazines. And next to the entertainment center were stacks of audio and videotapes.

Davie plunked down on the velvet couch and I sat down next to him. He started in talking, well rambling on. He sank deeper into the couch as I put my arms around him.

"I was just thinking. I was just thinking that I don't want to die. I'll take some treatments. I'll be back," he said as he trembled. "I'll beat this. I'll beat it like Clint Eastwood beats a drunken desperado. We'll build a house. We'll raise our children. I'll get a job. Maybe a job at the bank." He was talking in a candle blow voice as he took my hand, "I'll get a third opinion, a fourth. I can see it clearly now. I'm fit. I'm as strong as Arnold Schwartkough. I'll talk to God. God made me special. To perform for a hundred years like George Burns. I wrote *Wallowing Wuv.* I wrote *Brown Eyed Handsome Cow.* God, I'll make you a deal. I'll go back to church. I'll get my fourth annulment. I'll play hootenanny masses."

As Davie went on he seemed to go into one of those hallucinogenic things. "I'm flummoxed, discombobulated. Why didn't Otto stop me? Why didn't Michael stop me? I'm in a jam, in a stew. I'm going to Hell. Not just Hell, but the worst part of Hell. Just me and Jerry Springer at the bottom of Hell. I'm flying away in Apollo's chariot. We're flying into the sun. It's not Apollo's chariot. It's a '56 Thunderbird. It's James Dean and we're going to Odessa. Apollo, Odessa."

With that Davie fell dead asleep on the couch. I put one of my grandmother's appliquéd quilts over him and went off to bed.

Incidentally, Davie and I, we never had any children.

Chapter Eight
November 6, 1997
Green Bay, Wisconsin

A couple of hours later after I was sound asleep, Davie stirred and his despair came flooding back. His desire was to lay down and forget forever, however, his whole body was electrified and unconsciously compelled. Going into the bathroom, he took a large bottle of pills out of the medicine cabinet. He put on his coat and grabbed a guitar case out of living room. Before leaving the apartment he got a butcher knife from the kitchen and slipped it into the case next to the guitar. Out into the stinging November night he went, then cranked and cranked on his antiquated Tempo before it started. Expelled from his home by his deep desolation and thrust into the night, he squinted through the frosty windshield with no idea of his destination. He headed to the other side of town past his dad's dealership, no longer Fender Ford. Looking for a familiar niche, he studied the modern show room and expanded garage. Nothing familiar remained. He continued on into his old neighborhood noting every house and naming every family. Then he was in front of his boyhood home pulling over and stopping. It was as if he had just left. Maybe his folks were inside and in a few hours mom would be serving breakfast. He laid his head on the steering wheel and began crying as Otto and Helen were both in Heaven. Davie felt that he was on his way to join them in the here after, but most definitely not Heaven. In a blur of tears and memories he yanked the car back into drive and jerked it onto the street. With his eyes still stinging he stopped in front of St. Joseph's Catholic Church.

Guitar case in hand, Davie walked into the deathly quiet church. Streetlights glowed against the ornate stained glass windows and made the interior's outlines almost visible. A few flickering vigil lights danced off of the walls telling him this was truly the house of the Lord. Sensing that the church had changed over the last thirty years, Davie stood in the back until he had assimilated the changes. He proceeded to the front and stopped at the edge of the sanctuary. He opened the guitar case, and took out the butcher knife. He held it out in front of him and stared at it, then laid it on the front pew. With watery eyes and trembling hands he took out the guitar. Once that trusty Gibson was in his hands, the rest was automatic. He closed his eyes, felt her smooth neck and full hollow body, then strummed some gospel chords, da, da, da, dum, dum, dum. "Oh Lord, oh Lord," he started. "Oh please, dear Lord." Strumming softly da, da, da. "I know that I've done you wrong. I know I've sinned my share. I'll be with the devil tomorrow. Oh Lord, please Lord, I'm asking you to care." Da, da, da, dum, dum, dum, "I'm just asking you to care." Da, da, da, d, d, he tried to strum as exhaustion finally prevailed. Curling up on the front pew, he drifted off to sleep.

******

Early the next morning, as the faint autumn sun struggled to illuminate the Jacob's Ladder mosaic on the stained glass window, Davie was still sleeping. Making her rounds of the grounds at that time was St. Joseph's last remaining nun, Sister Mary Lynn.

Packing more punch than a Gilbert Brown forearm the ageless Sister Mary Sunshine had originally come to St. Joseph's as a History and English teacher. She agreed to become the Principal of the High School when the former principal was asked to leave because he mixed too much Vodka with the holy water. She had taken over the parish's struggling day care program a few years ago and cut back to being Assistant Principal. In addition to her formal positions, she had a number of other duties, such as making sure the church was freshened up for each new day.

As Sister Mary Lynn entered the house of God, she first noticed Davie's guitar case and went up the aisle to investigate. Sister was shocked to find a man sleeping in one of her pews. And a butcher knife. She quickly picked up the knife and put it up the sleeve of her coat.

She reached over and tapped Davie on the shoulder. "Sir, Sir it's morning."

"Oh, my God!" said a surprised Davie looking up at the sprightly munchinesque nun with sparkling blue eyes.

"No, actually I'm Sister Mary Lynn."

"Oh my Sister, I'm Davie Fender."

"I've heard of you."

"Really?"

"You're Davie Fender, the annulment guy. "Where are you going?"

"Actually I'm dying and I'm headed to Hell."

"Why did you stop here?"

"This used to be my parish and I need a miracle."

"Most people come during the day."

"I'm mostly up at night."

"What do you do?"

"I'm a musician. I used to be the country star. I was wishing I was already dead."

"Nonsense, you need to believe in the Lord. You must believe in yourself. You must live every day to the fullest," she bubbled with her Julia Child's enthusiasm.

"I lived every night to the fullest," he said lowering his gaze.

" What you have to offer is valuable," she continued, trying to look him in the eye.

"Have you ever heard of *Brown Eyed Handsome Cow?*" Davie asked.

"Yes, isn't that the most moronic song you've ever heard."

Davie buried his face in his hands and emitted a hideous noise somewhere between a moan and a scream.

"Now, now Mr. Fender let's pray together."

"Would you say something in Latin for me. Latin is so reassuring."

Sister Mary Lynn started, "In nominee Patris et Filii et Spiritus Sancti, Amen." She continued saying the Pater Noster in Latin, with Davie joining in for a sporadic word here and there that he vaguely remembered from his altar boy days.

"It's so good to hear the real language of Catholicism. But I'm sure I'm still going to Hell."

"I see you spending a lot of time in Purgatory while a committee reviews your case."

"What are the chances of getting Jimi Hendrix and Janis Joplin on my committee?"

"I don't know how those committees are chosen. They are other musicians, aren't they?"

"They would truly be a jury of my peers."

"Here's a strategy for you to use. It's called the Apiori Defense. God usually comes around when a good soul uses the Apiori Defense."

"What's the Apriori Defense?"

"It's based on Apriori Knowledge."

"What's Apriori Knowledge?"

"That means knowing something before you knew that you knew it."

"Is that good?"

"It can be super good, if you play it right. You had Apriori Knowledge of God, which is very virtuous. It proves that you were always in search of God."

"Sometimes I was in search of other things."

"No, you just thought you were in search of other things. Remember, tell God you were in search of him but you didn't know where to look."

"Like State Fair."

"Whatever."

"So how does that Apriori thing work?" he asked, putting his hopes in the little nun.

"Yours were sins of familiarity. God is very quick to forgive familiar sins."

"You mean like looking for love in all the old places?"

"Remember the Old Testament and God's chosen people. They all had Apriori Knowledge, and in the end, he always worked a deal for them."

"Yes, a Plenary Indulgence," Davie called out as he remembered the concept out of his catechism.

"Exactly."

"I just remembered. I bought piles of Pagan Babies when I was in Catholic School. They should count for something."

"I'm sure all of those Pagan Babies are praying for you now."

"Have you ever met any of those Pagan Babies?"

"I went on a world tour in 1987. I'd say some of the people I met were pagan."

"No, I mean the ones we bought out of paganism with our dimes and nickels."

"Oh sure. Oh, I'm sure I met some of them."

"Were they appreciative?"

"Oh yes, being free of paganism was the most unforgivable, I mean unforgettable, thing that ever happened to them."

"That's so reassuring to hear. You have been so good to me. I know a Juan B. Fine song that's sort of about a conversation, kind of like we've just had. It's called *Chewing the Fat is Where it's At* and I'd like to sing it for you."

Davie took his guitar out of the case, began strumming, and then remembered the knife. A nun, a knife? Turning ruby red for an instant, he quickly glanced right and left, then straight ahead for a few seconds. Strumming the guitar, he continued,

"When I have filled my brain
With pure grain alcohol
I look up my old girl friend
And just give her a call.
We just hash it over
We just chew the ham.
Then after two whole minutes
She tells me to scram.

I am so disgusting
I don't know where I'm at.
I just need somebody
To sit and chew the fat.

When I have filled my circuits
With white California wine.
I just dial 900
And I am feeling fine.
We just talk it over and
We just chew the lard.
And the voice on the other end
Only wants my credit card.

I am so disgusting
I don't know where I'm at.
I just need somebody
To sit and chew the fat.

When I have filled my mind
With Puerto Rican Rum
I run out at mid night
And yell up to the sun.
I just shout all over
I just chew the beef.
And a voice from up above says
Why give me your grief?

I am so disgusting
I don't know where I'm at.
I just need somebody
To sit and chew the fat."

Chapter Nine
December 10, 1997
Green Bay, Wisconsin

It had been a month since we learned that Davie had cancer, causing a constant whir of doctor's appointments and clinic visits. It was exhausting and I began having this recurring nightmare. There I was in the dream, a younger me dressed in those dorky clothes that I wore as a teenager, out in a field searching for something. But I didn't know what I was hunting for. In every direction I tried I became more and more confused. I wanted to run but I was heavy in mud that practically paralyzed me. The flowers of the field transformed from being beautiful to looking hideous. The bushes started growing up around me and blocking my movement. Trapped and terrified, I would always awake in a panic.

We spent Thanksgiving Day with my parents. In some ways it was good and in other ways it was not. My dad told his ten jokes and laughed for exactly three seconds after each one. It was pretty hard to laugh along after having heard them hundreds of times. I barely picked at the sun-tanned turkey that Mom had prepared. She found it a little annoying, but deep down I think she understood. Of course, mom was bragging about my last promotion at the bank, even though it had been several years ago. They were so concerned about Davie that the conversation seemed to contain nothing but cancer. Had we tried this? Had we done that? Did we think that maybe this was the time to get married? With every question they asked, I sunk. Finally, I made up some lame excuse about laundry and we beat it out of there.

Having a cup of coffee for breakfast and a bagel for lunch, I very quickly dropped fifteen pounds. I had thoughts of Davie and I in his old Tempo. That was strange because we always used my newer Bronco. We were driving along and suddenly hit head on. Both gone together. Those thoughts left me shaking and I tried to quickly find something else to do.

Davie on the other hand was rebounding. After a week of throwing his music magazines around the apartment and moaning "Why me," he started feeling better. He talked about that night in the church with Sister Lynn, saying he had never experienced such deep despair. We began going to Saturday afternoon mass where occasionally he'd see Sister. And he seriously considered going to confession; however, Roy kept joking that it would be a Guinness world record confession. He started making notes for me about what to do in case he was not around. He said he wanted to tidy up his life. Ironically, he also started tidying up the apartment. Martha Stewart would have been proud.

On Friday and Saturday nights the boys kept playing at The Dog. Of course Roy and Michael never let up with the wise cracks nor acted differently, even when my leathery man started losing his hair. They went on as if he was going to lick it. It was baldy this and baldy that. Davie even took Roy some of his hair. I had lost fifteen pounds and these guys were still slap sticking around. I knew even then that Roy would find some way to turn a buck with that hair.

And one other little thing happened at that time. My here-to-fore hearth bound hero became determined to travel to Austin and meet the Pope. He thought the Pope would grant him a plenary indulgence. At first that meant nothing to me. Now I know all about plenary indulgences. They are like the Elvis Presley of all indulgences. No matter what you've done wrong, God can not say no to a plenary indulgence. Davie believed he needed someone of power or influence to get him to Austin. Michael called Larry Tacoma several times and the answer was always the same. They had absolutely no news of the Pope coming to Austin.

As it so happened, my bank was one of many banks owned by The Bush Conglomerate out of Austin. Through Davie's own personal skewed conjuration, he believed that talking to someone at my bank would be his ticket to *Austin City Limits*. Now my boss was Donald J. Groan, Senior Vice President. Shall we say he's a little on the stuffy side. He was also the man that got me promoted out of the loan department. Davie wanted to meet with him in the worst way. Anyway, what's an hour of his time. He'd just be down in the officer's lounge practicing his putting. He was delighted to do me the favor.

VP Groan's office was larger than Davie had expected. On his other visits to the bank he was always accommodated in one of our tiny drab bankruptcy rooms. The walls in my boss' office were decorated in lifeless architectural drawings. And there were dozens of high-backed walnut chairs everywhere around the room. Don Groan was dressed in an impeccable business suit, seated behind his walnut desk in the highest of high-backed chairs.

"Come in Mr. Fender. Have a chair, any chair." greeted a solemn Mr. Groan.

"It's good to see you again," said Davie. I believe the last time was the house repossession, or was it the truck?"

"Yes, those were the good old days," he groaned. "I'm sorry to hear about your illness. I imagine that you are here to talk to Mrs. Mourning over in estate planning."

"No, I really don't need estate planning."

"I don't know how you do it," moans Groan. "You are the only person in Green Bay without a personal certified financial consultant."

"I have a savings account and a checking account. What else is there?"

"Davie, you'll be happy to know that the bank contacted T - Bone Recording Studios and we are using one of your songs."

"Which one?"

"If you call the bank and unfortunately get put on hold, which hardly ever happens because we are the friendliest bank in the valley, you will hear *Momma Teach Your Babies to Grow Up and Be Packers* as sung by The Purple Haze. They're a real country band."

"I see," said Davie, as the thought to himself, this guy couldn't find the country music section of Best Buy with Superman leading the way.

"Are you still getting royalties off of that song?"

"Yes, about two dollars a month."

"You're right. You don't need estate planning," said the VP as he glanced at this watch. "Go ahead. I want to help in any way I can. Marion is one of our best employees. And your father was a capital asset to this community. No one holds him personally responsible for those Pintos. Who was to know. So, how can I help you?"

"Now your bank is owned by the Bush Conglomerate which is headquartered in Austin, right?" asked Davie.

"That's right. I went there a couple of years ago for a barbeque," Groan paused, "and banking symposium, naturally."

"Does your conglomerate support Public Television?"

"I'm not sure where you're going with that question. But we support everything good."

"Do you support specifically Public Television?"

"Yes, you've come to the right place. We have a large education area in the basement. You have seen our new ads on TV. They say we are the friendliest bank in the valley."

"I don't want to go to the education area," Davie protested, wondering how does one talk the talk of a Senior Vice President.

"Just let me know what you want and I'd be more than happy to send you along."

"What can you do personally?"

"I'm a vice president. I don't do anything. I supervise people who really do things. That's why the sooner I find out what you need the sooner I can move you along to one of the friendliest employees in the valley," said a determined Mr. Groan, grinding his elbows into the desk.

"I want to meet the Pope."

"Good. That's easy enough," said Don Groan as he reached for the phone. "I'll arrange for that. I'll call Avis over in our travel loan section. She'll see you immediately. I'm sure we can loan you the money to fly to Rome. We're always on the side of right. That's the far side of right."

"No, let me explain," Davie blurted out as Groan abruptly hung up the phone. "The Pope is coming to America."

"No he isn't. I would know that."

"Nobody knows yet."

"I've heard you started chemotherapy. Has that effected your mind?"

"Really, Michael and I got an inside tip."

"Davie Fender, notorious pot head, knows, but no one else does. Excuse me Mr. Fender, what I meant was how interesting, an inside tip."

"Actually the Pope is coming to Austin."

'Not Los Angeles and not New York, but Austin. Are you stoned again on some of that Acupuncture Gold?"

"No! I'm totally sober."

"Did Roy Ryman put you up to this?"

"No, No, No, I'm totally serious. The Pope is going to appear on Austin City Limits."

"Haaaaaa. Haaaaa." The most somber man in the Midwest exploded into fits of laughter. "Owwww! The Pope is appearing on a hillbilly music show. Ohhhh. Excuse me. Oh, excuse me. I don't laugh often so I'm a little out of practice." He sputtered as he attempted to regain an upright position. "Let's just pretend for a minute that The Pope is going to be in Austin. You could drive there. Well, not in your car." He tittered at his little joke. "But Marion has a new Bronco."

"Is this the friendliest bank in the valley? I don't think you understand."

"Au contraire, I understand. You don't want estate planning. You don't want a travel loan. You don't want informational pamphlets. You don't want a car loan. And where you're going you don't need a home loan. We're running out of services to offer you."

"I need help."

"You've always needed help. You have a history of using all of your discretionary income on indiscretion."

"No, help to see The Pope."

"Why are we back to that?"

"Because I have a plan. My plan is that you talk to headquarters in Austin and let them in on this. They become an underwriter for the show and give you a big promotion. At the last minute headquarters tells KLRU, oh, we have another condition. That condition being Davie Fender gets to meet The Pope. Just for a minute."

"Davie, Davie that's not how things are done in the real world. My position here only gives me the authority to talk to the Head Teller in Austin. If The Pope really went to Austin their stadium would be totally filled with big oil executives. The only one meeting The Pope would be Monica Lewinski."

"I don't believe that. He would reach out to the common people."

"Davie, the secret to life is business. Big business. In the ledger of life you've frittered away all of your assets. Business sells everything to everybody. It runs the art world, the same as it runs government. Like those royalties you get."

"It doesn't run religion."

"Have you seen cable television?"

"Business doesn't control education."

"Why does your friend Roy Ryman want to open a charter school?"

"That was a joke."

"That's what we told him," Don Groan continued. "Davie, everything is big business. Faith, Hope, and Charity. Pride, covetousness, and lust. Sympathy, privacy, and loyalty. Honesty and beauty are all big business."

"What about the occult, the metaphysical, and UFOs?"

"Mystically, turned into big business. Air and water, light and dark, they're all big business."

"Don, you're telling me darkness is big business."

"Davie, just this week I invested ten grand in a blindingly simple idea. Dark Sky Preserves will undoubtedly make me a millionaire. We have so much man made light there is a glaring need for darkness. It's like drive in movies without the overhead. Anybody who wants to see the moon or stars has to go through us. It's impossible to stub one's toe on an investment like that."

"Well like you say, I don't need any more darkness where I'm going. Isn't there anyone at your bank who can help? Can't you kick this upstairs to your boss?"

"I'm going to go to the man that controls my future and tell him that Davie Fender, noted druggie, no offense intended, has an inside tip that the Pope is going to appear on an outback music show. The only thing I can think of that would be worse would be spending a night at The Howling Dog Saloon."

"I don't think that this is the time for name calling. If you ask me, Cheese Head National Bank is a pretty tacky name for a bank."

Davie stood to leave and put out his hand to shake with the VP. Instead of shaking hands with Davie, Don shoved a business card into his open hand.

"Davie, if you do see the Pope, give him my card. Tell him we're not money changers. We're the friendliest bank in the valley."

Chapter Ten
January 9, 1998
Green Bay, Wisconsin

Davie muttered over his disappointing meeting with Don Groan for about five minutes, but then he was off to "brain storm with his think tank." Of course that meant gabbing with Roy and Michael. Roy reasoned that if Davie were elected mayor of Austin they would have to invite him. Michael suggested that they contact T - Bone Recording Studios, the producers of their three almost hit records. Contact with T -Bone over the last few years had been scant, just annual reports and things like that. Michael had recently received a letter saying that a young yearling rep was their new contact person. That was the first I heard of Jamie Napster, whom the boys told me looked like a fifteen-year-old Robert Goulet.

Several phone calls later, Michael had arranged for Jamie to fly to Green Bay. It was all set, a businessman's luncheon between Davie and Jamie at the city's premiere country eating establishment.

It was colder than a three dog night when Jamie's plane touched down at Austin Staubel Field. They had stopped deicing the planes twenty degrees ago since the air was too cold to hold any moisture. Michael was dispatched to the airport to pick up Jamie as the heater in Davie's Tempo only worked on an intermittent basis; therefore making it safer to send Maki.

"We call this the Hawk," Michael explained to the shivering young rep, who was trying desperately to wrap his arms around his overcoat.

Jamie uttered not a word of reply because he believed his lips to be frozen closed. He struggled to pull his overcoat tighter and stared at the polar landscape with eyes the size of snowballs.

Michael pulled into Kroll's Cholesterol Cathedral and picked up a huge bag of their lipsmacking butter burgers. Once the cuisine was secure, the calf and the veal were delivered to The Dog.

"Jumpin' Jimminie is it always this cold up here?" asked the frostbitten rep, who was trying to feel his way while walking on numb tingling stubs.

"Almost always. Except February is colder," answered Davie. "I'm Davie Fender and this is Roy Ryman, owner of this country music Mecca," as they shook hands all around.

"Wow, Mr. Ryman, this is just like a museum in here. And I'm not just saying that because you have heat in here. You've got pictures of Patsy Cline and Kitty Wells. There's the old blue grass king himself, Bill Monroe. And Flatt and Scruggs. You can't hardly find pictures of them any more."

"This place has been called a lot of things, but never a museum. I like that."

"Look at that Christmas tree. It looks a little singed."

"Hadn't noticed that," replied Roy, not wanting to get into the story of beer dousing, which would not be a fitting function for a museum.

"All of those ornaments have beer names and logos. And baby Jesus is holding a can of Miller Lite. How appropriate."

"A museum. That has possibilities. I've set up a table with everything. I'll be in back if you need anything else."

The table was perfectly located between Dolly Parton and Kenny Rogers, and lighted by a plastic Tiffany chandelier that touted Chippewa Beer. Davie had great expectations.

"Yes, Mr. Fender, I wish I had a picture of this place to show the other agents."

"How long have you worked for T - Bone Studios?"

"I've only been there a year Mr. Fender but I know all about you. You're notorious, I mean famous, at T - Bone.

"Famous?"

"Yes, they say that no one ever got more notoriety with three songs than you did."

"It probably has something to do with my personal appearances."

"Oh yes Mr. Fender, those are all the buzz. Did you really autograph people with Crisco at Fan Fare?"

"Young man it's hard to know where fact leaves off and legend takes over."

"Well I think I should tell you I don't smoke pot."

"That's okay. Everybody in Green Bay does, but we're mighty tolerant toward outsiders."

"That's what I thought. That's what I told my boss. Actually, my boss didn't want me to come. He said peculiar things happen when you're around," frothed the frosty rep as he pulled his coat collar up around his ears.

"Jamie that's just more legend."

"My boss said that the only things that Green Bay people know are fishing and bowling. And he said, in the winter it's too cold to go fishing."

"That's preposterous. He said that about the good people of Green Bay? Absolutely absurd. It's never too cold to go fishing. Haven't you heard of ice fishing? We take shanties out onto the ice so we can fish all year round. I'll have Michael show you some on the way back to the airport."

"Mr. Fender, I really wanted to meet you. I mean I really wanted to meet you before you die. Michael explained to me how ill you are."

"Thank you. I've got one last project I want to accomplish."

"I've never worked with a dying client before and I'm a little nervous."

"I've never been a dying client before, so that makes two of us."

"You know why I wanted to meet you?" asked Jamie, as he kept repositioning and rotating his butter burger trying to make it fit into his mouth.

"No."

"Because of *Wallowing Wuv,*" Jamie sputtered through a mouthful of bun and burger.

"You liked that song?"

"A couple of years ago when I was in grad school, I was totally stymied. I was stuck in this redolent relationship. She was a swine sent from above; just like you said in the song. Your song captured the whole stinking situation for me. I was wallowing for months. And it was your song that finally got me out of it."

"Wow. I must confess, I was slightly stoned when I wrote that."

"Hey, what are poets for? I didn't realize that you had written it until I started working for T - Bone. They had one of your old records. Imagine that, a record. What do you call that style?"

"Dairylang Twang."

"It's sure smoother than a bowl of grits."

So there they were happier than Jennie Craig at an alfalfa buffet. Slurping slippery bulky burgers. Fingering fatty fries and eating salad out of flimsy containers. The old songsmith and the greenhorn smiled at each other as the butter dripped off their chins.

"So, Mr. Fender what can I do for you? We assumed that you've written a song to reflect back on your life and would like T - Bone to produce it for you."

"It's not really that simple. I'm looking for someone with a little influence to get Maki and I on *Austin City Limits.*"

"You've come to the right place. I have very little influence. Have you tried calling Austin?"

"Michael has called, written, sent demo tapes. All to no avail."

"Maybe if you told them you were dying."

"You mean like *Survivor*? Actually I want to get on one particular show. The Pope is going to be on *Austin City Limits* June 20th."

"How do you know that? Only a few top insiders know that."

"Are you a top insider?"

"No, but I work with some top insiders."

"So maybe the word is dribbling out," said Davie as he wiped his chin.

"Here's everything I know about it. *The Grand Ole Opry* has approached The Vatican with their offer. *Austin City Limits* wants Neil Mc Coy as the headliner for the show. It's real political and I doubt you stand a chance of getting near the building."

"How about discussing this with the top beef at T-Bone?"

"Mr. Fender, the top bulls at the studio are still suffering a little distemper over *Brown Eyed Handsome Cow*," Jamie started hesitantly, not wanting to offend his hero. "You have to admit it wasn't a conventional kind of cow song. A song about a cross bred, cross eyed, cross dressing cow, that criss-crossed the country wearing a cross your heart bra. The transsexual, transspecies, and transcontinental themes offended a whole herd of people."

"So what did you think?"

"I was an undergrad at Texas A&M when I first heard it. I automatically thought it was written by Weird Al."

"I wrote it after I had a nightmare about state fair."

"So those state fair stories are true?"

"Just more legend Jamie."

"The top dogs, as you call them, showed me the file on *Brown Eyed Handsome Cow*. The Cattleman's Association would have gone after you like they did Oprah, but everybody knows you're broke."

"Lucky for me."

"The Kansas City Livestock Board demanded songs that projected positive images about cows. Songs where the cows would be the celebrity by saving the city or getting the girl."

"Udderly unimaginable."

"The Chicago Beef Exchange approached every company they could. They wanted super hero cows. Action figure cows. They wanted video games about cows."

"Really? That song caused that much fuss?"

"Yes Mr. Fender. If you hadn't been stuck up here in Green Bay, you could have been a revolutionary like Bob Dylan or John Lennon."

"Unbelievable!"

"Ever thought of taking one of those Woody Guthrie melodies, putting it together with your dairylang twang and telling your life story?"

"Not really. I've just got to find some way to meet the Pope and gain forgiveness."

"I don't think *Brown Eyed Handsome Cow* was that bad."

"Not just that Jamie, there were other things."

"What other things Mr. Fender?"

"It would take another two months. And that would be just for the truth, not the legend. It's almost time for Michael to pick you up," said Davie, as he glanced at the flickering lights on the Blatz display.

Jamie had never taken off his coat, so getting ready to go was easy.

"Thank you for the lunch Mr. Fender. Those burgers were juicier than a Kinky Friedman mystery. It's been an honor to meet you."

"Stay warm buddy," said Davie, as Jamie clutched his hand.

"You too, Mr. Fender. I mean, as long as you're in Green Bay."

Chapter Eleven
January 14, 1998
Green Bay, Wisconsin

A few days after his meeting with Jamie Napster, Davie phoned Sister Mary Lynn, who invited him to visit her at the convent. He grabbed a guitar, threw it in his vintage Tempo and shivered his way over to the convent. The eternally upbeat Sister Mary Lynn met him with the warmest of welcomes, a definite contrast to the spartan surroundings of the convent living room. Davie sat in a faded fully stuffed cocoa brown parlor chair, under an old-fashioned picture of the Blessed Virgin with a blue-violet heart radiating from her chest. He felt a great calmness being with his sister savior.

"I appreciate the invitation. I hope we can pray together," said Davie taking off his stocking cap and exposing his bald head.

"I was hoping we could talk some time. I found out you are semi-famous around Green Bay," continued Sister with a puckered pious smile.

"By semi-famous you mean I'm neither Reggie White nor Brett Favre, but a few people have heard of me?"

"No, I mean you wrote *Brown Eyed Handsome Cow*. And I think I said it wasn't one of my favorites."

"No, you called it moronic," Davie laughed and slouched down into the over stuffed heirloom.

"I probably did. M-o-r-o-n-i-c. I like using that word. And you still want us to pray together?"

"That's not bad. One fellow thought it was written by Weird Al."

"I do like *Wallowing Wuv*. It makes me glad I joined the convent."

"Why are so few women joining the convent?"

"I think sacrifice has lost its appeal. There are so many ways to suffer without becoming a nun. There are tattoos and piercings."

"I never thought of that. I figured it was the vow of silence."

"Did you write other songs?"

"I wrote *Momma Teach Your Babies To Grow Up And Be Packers*."

"I heard that the other day on the phone."

"Your bank?"

"Yes. How did you know that?"

"I get a small royalty off of it. Very small."

"Did you write other songs?"

"I started one about Rhinelander one time, but never finished it."

"What a beautiful subject. That Oneida County just takes my breath away. The majestic pines and the fragrant cedars. Lake Tomahawk is one of the most pristine I've ever seen. And Lake Nokomis is pure bliss. So how did your song go?"

Davie remembered all to well about The Rhinelanderer Philanderer, but wasn't about to show a glimpse of recognition for his favorite nun. "Gee, that's a long time ago. It's hard to remember. Ah-h-h, it was about a Rhinelanderer Wanderer. Ya, it's about a guy who loved nature and traveled over the mountains and into the valleys. He went from bush to bush and reveled in the beauties of nature, sort of."

"I bet it would have been like the coolest. But I didn't remember there were mountains up there. You probably wonder why I'm talking so much about songs. I started writing a song once. My father worked in the paper mills. I wanted to write about being a paper mill workers daughter. Would you like to hear what I have done so far?"

"Of course. I even have my guitar and could play along."

"You'd better wait until you hear it," Sister cautioned.

"My daddy worked in the mill,
Up on the hill,
Next to his still,
But it paid the bill.

"That's the beginning. We didn't live on a hill. And goodness gracious we didn't have a still. That's poetic license," said the suddenly very self-conscious little nun.

Davie thought to himself, that's poetic assault and battery. "That's a g-good start. Are you going to continue?" he asked.

"Now I'm looking for words that rhyme with Kelvinator."

"Even if you don't become a famous song writer. You're a good nun, and a great person."

"Thank you. I pray for you every day. I even have a gift for you," she said, looking more serious than Davie had remembered ever seeing her.

She left the room and returned in a minute carrying a brown paper bag that was all rolled up in a long narrow clump. "I found this the same night that I found you," she said. "You don't need to open it now."

There was a very loud moment of silence as she handed Davie the package. He could feel the knife through the brown paper wrapping.

"Thank you," he said very softly.

"I didn't want you to think that I had habits worse than song writing," she added in order to try and soften the edge of the moment.

"See you later alligator," Davie replied.

"Are you leaving so soon?" she asked fearing that the return of the knife had scared him off.

"No, See you later Alligator rhymes with Kelvinator."

"Wowie zowie, I'll have to use that," she said and clasped her in joy that he was staying for a longer visit.

"Being a nun and everything, I have some news I bet you'll find interesting," Davie began spewing as he launched into the entire story about how his partner Michael, this Type A positive personality, was determined to get them on *Austin City Limits*. He provided her with all of the details about Maki calling Austin, Archbishop Nelson, and his listening in to their private conversation. Davie continued telling her about his professional encounter with Don Groan, and his follow up businessman's luncheon meeting with Jamie Napster. At each turn, Sister became more amazed that this well-worn warrior she had found in her church was in the middle of such an interesting episode.

"That Archbishop Nelson sure must be some kind of egomaniac," Davie continued.

"He always has been," Sister asserted.

"What do you mean, he always has been?'

"He's a friend of mine," said Sister as Davie's nerves crackled, and he worried that he had offended her.

"I meant he's a pious egomaniac."

Sister put her hand reassuringly on Davie's shoulder. "No, Bobby Nelson has always been a plain old egomaniac. I like that word e-g-o-m-a-n-i-a-c."

"How do you know the Archbishop?"

"We grew up together. Went to the same Catholic grade school. We were both attracted to religion, but I think for different reasons. He was always the biggest kid in class and a smooth talker. Like that Bill Clinton. We got reacquainted when he was a Bishop in Chicago. He would come to Green

Bay and we'd visit. He said it was to check on the Pagan Babies, but he always found time to slip over to the Packer's practice field. Other times he'd go golfing. He's a terrible golfer you know. That story you told sounded just like him. He'd be a good one to organize the Pope's visit."

"This sounds delusional, but could you talk to him for me?"

"D-e-l-u-s-i-o-n-a-l, another good word. It would be moronic not to squeak up to the egomaniac for you. Why don't you take out that guitar and play something while I make a phone call."

Davie started strumming and singing.
"Lord help me if you can,
Lordy, lordy I am your man.
Lord help me if you can,
Put the Pope in my plan."

Sister Lynn searched her antique Rolodex and in minutes was dialing the Archbishop. Davie stopped playing and listened to her end of the conversation from the adjoining room. "This is Lynn Washington, Sister Mary Lynn. Yes, I got your Christmas card. I guess that's how they think of Christmas in Texas. Yes, quite unique. I heard that the Pope might be coming to America. Do you know anything about that?" She paused. "It's pure speculation. I heard that he might come to Texas." She listened. "You say it's just a rumor. I heard he might come to Austin." She paused again. "Very tentative, you say. That's interesting, I heard he's appearing on *Austin City*

Limits on June 20^(th)." Sister Mary Lynn immediately moved the receiver away from her ear.

From all the way in the next room, Davie heard the boom damn, boom damn, boom damn coming from the phone.

Sister Lynn continued, "I take that as a yes. Are you in charge of planning?" She listened. "It's supposed to be top secret. It's going to be announced in two weeks. What is the chance to get a good Catholic boy in to see the Pope? Impossible."

Davie had started sweating. How could he get such a break, he thought. Sister Mary Lynn actually knowing the Archbishop. But sometimes it's better when things are so remote that they are totally impossible. That may be better than having them inches away but still unobtainable.

Sister Lynn continued, "This is someone who could add to the Pope's visit. He has an almost nationally known country band called The Word. He plays one h-heck of a fiddle. He used to play hootenanny masses here at St. Joe's." She listened at his less than enthusiastic reply.

"His father was a leader in the lay ministry here and a big contributor." With still no hint that the Archbishop was coming around, Sister continued. "This man has cancer and a good chance of not surviving. He's undergoing chemotherapy and has lost all of his hair. His last wish is to meet the Pope."

Davie listened intently but Sister seemed to be getting nowhere.

"Think back to when you were coordinating the Pagan Babies?" She continued. "I believe you owe me a favor from those days. And this young man bought the most Pagan Babies of anyone in Green Bay. Do you remember him?"

The Archbishop remembered that he owed the little nun. He also remembered who bought the most Pagan Babies. That person had made him the top Pagan Baby Coordinator in the country, which won for him his first free trip to the Vatican. Unfortunately, he remembered the student's name and it wasn't Davie Fender.

"You always said if you could do anything to help that young man you would," Sister continued. "Bobby, we share a common dogma. We celebrate the resurrection of the one true Christ. We have the common bonds of celibacy and chastity. I see Jesus looking down from the cross at you and saying 'Nellie you owe me'. If you grant me this one miracle, we'll roll back the stones of Easter Sunday forever. You'll be totally forgiven."

She put down the receiver and walked back into the living room. Her bearing was poker straight and offered Davie no clue. She paused, and Davie blurted out, "I didn't realize I remembered the Our Father. I think I said a hundred of them. What did he say?"

"He's going to get you an audience with the Pope, but he thinks your name is Johnny Lee Linton."

Chapter Twelve
February 2, 1998
Green Bay, Wisconsin

Ground Hog Day in Wisconsin is something sacred. We've already had five months of winter, and any slight hope that it will end before July is very welcome. In other parts of the world they celebrate. We pray. Last Ground Hog Day we had reason to pray and celebrate. Sister Mary Lynn had had some follow up conversations with the Archbishop and he was going to try and get the boys an appearance on the show. Davie's treatments were going well; he was almost pain free and he felt stronger. He and Michael continued performing at The Howling Dog. I was sleeping better, not dreaming and gaining back a few pounds. It was either that or buy a new wardrobe. Davie had telephoned Sister a dozen times to thank her. I told him that maybe his calling was getting a little annoying. Roy thought they should hold a special function at The Dog in her honor. He was going to call it 'A Night to Have Fun with a Nun'. I talked them into sending her a fruit basket.

Now here is the quizzical part. Davie was feeling bad about smoking marijuana. He had been smoking pot for thirty years without a tinge of guilt. Then, when it made medical sense to smoke a little medical marijuana, his conscience turned on him. I tried to tell him to stop fretting. I told him God had found him the cure before he had found him the illness. A mere thirty years.

There we were on February Second sitting around Roy's bar and listening to him tell us the facts of life. "The sin markets have closed. Let's go over to our own bull with a snort full, market guru, Jack Daniels." Roy continued with an attempt at a turgid accent, "We have all the news from the DOW and the S and P. Beer was down two burps and a belch. Whiskey was off a fifth. This year women seem to prefer traditional turkeys, like their husbands, to Wild Turkey. The only good news was in hallucinogenics, which were unchanged. However, everyone said they saw them rise. In the futures market, Davie is high on hemp. The S and P, other wise known as the Slang and Profanity Index was hotter than Madonna, following the lead of *MTV* and *VH-1*. The DOW, meaning Decadence of Wisconsin Index, remains volatile due to the recent merger of PM with S. Casino attendance was down during the Christmas holidays as cookie decorating and tree trimming were added to most nursing home schedules." Roy stopped and held out his hands waiting for the applause, and of course, I applauded. The boys threw popcorn.

"Roy, you are truly the strangest of red headed strangers," said Michael.

"You boys love it. Davie even waited to light up until I was done. You need somebody like me to go along with you to Austin. If you get tongue tied, I'd talk to the Pope for you."

"We don't even know what's going to happen yet," Michael said. It could be Davie going with Marion. Or should I say Johnny Lee going with Marion."

"I have a strong feeling Nellie's going to get us on the show," said Davie.

"Oh so now its Nellie?" Asked Michael.

"So, what if the Pope gives a plenary indulgence to someone he thinks is Johnny Lee, who really gets the indulgence?" quipped Roy.

"I get the indulgence Roy. A real Catholic knows those things," said Davie, making the same kind of corny face at Roy that he does when he beats him to the electrical plug.

"Only you could get yourself into a fix like this with your old friend Johnny Lee," said Michael.

"I couldn't believe it when Sister Lynn said Johnny Lee. I thought I had heard the last of him when the Paper Company found his dad fondling more than the Charmin," said Davie.

"Why do you dislike that guy so much?" asked Roy.

"It wasn't so much him as what he stood for."

"So, what did he stand for?" asked Roy.

"Over achieving. He was one of those disgusting over achievers, present company excluded. He was a straight A suck up. He dressed like an Eskimo version of Liberace. Several times people told me that maybe I should be more like Johnny Lee. That's what really got me. Of course he would be the one who bought the most Pagan Babies. He was nauseating. Probably still is."

"That's the way I remember him," said Michael.

"So it had nothing to do with the two of you competing at the Riverside Ballroom?" asked Roy.

"You know I thoroughly kicked his paper products all of the way back to Lake Winnebago."

While regularly performing as Buzzards by The Bay, Michael and Davie had about a one year run at the old Riverside Ballroom. One hot summer night during their intermission, Davie had disappeared outside to down some boilermakers. Johnny Lee jumped onto the stage and started jiggling the ole piano to the amazement of most. The greasers and bobby soxers were really grooving on his music but the Buzzards were pissed. When the word of this got back to the owner of the Riverside he signed the boys and Johnny Lee up for a couple of 'Battles of the Bands'. Johnny Lee was almost as good a performer as Davie. And maybe if somebody were in love with Johnny they'd rate him a little better than Davie.

"So, do I get to go or not?" asked Roy for the umpteen hundredth time.

"Roy, I don't really care if you go," said Davie. "But I don't want to hear about the Riverside Ballroom. Hey, anyway it's up to Michael."

"We don't know yet that The Word is going," said Michael.

As you can see, Davie wanted Roy to go and Michael was holding back. The next week Roy sent bountiful spring bouquets to Valerie, Michael's wife, and myself. No explanation included.

The boys finally got the phone call they were waiting for. Sister Lynn had heard from the Archbishop and he said that he could get them on the show. She said that Nelson liked the fact that their band was known as The Word because of the religious significance. He just needed to work out a few technical details with Austin. Roy continued angling to go. He even increased their wages. I bet that hurt. So, Michael finally gave in. He said that Roy could join them if he agreed to be their roadie. Roadie Roy. He was to be their first, last and only roadie.

Then Davie got the phone call from Sister that no one expected. It seems that a couple of national magazines did write-ups on the Archbishop and his pivotal role in organizing the Pope's visit. A couple of parishioners remembered Bishop Nelson and called the convent to see if it was the same person. Then Sister got a call from Atlanta. It was the real Johnny Lee Linton wanting to know if she had the Archbishop's phone number. That Sister Mary Lynn was one cool customer. She got real chatty with him to find out everything she could. It seemed he had a couple more avenues to reach the Archbishop if she didn't have the number. She put it together pretty quickly that it was better for her to be involved and try to control it. But Johnny Lee wanted a ticket to the show and was prepared to make more calls to get it. She told Johnny Lee that she would call the Archbishop for him. Then she called Davie. Let's say he went slightly insane. He didn't want to see Johnny Lee ever again, but he understood that Johnny could trash the whole plan if he talked to the Archbishop. Over the next couple of days Davie feasted on humble pie. They agreed that Sister needed to call him back and tell him he had a ticket. They would figure out the rest later. Sister Lynn and Davie were on the phone every night hatching their plan. She is one clever woman, and will probably be the first woman Bishop. Sister Lynn told Johnny Lee that he needed to be in Austin a couple of days early to pick up his ticket. That was almost the truth. He really needed to meet Michael and Davie so he could become the third member of The Word. He was going to be their tambourine player; he just didn't know that yet. The boys figured they'd let him know at the opportune time.

Chapter Thirteen
April 15, 1998
San Antonio, Texas

Just above the absolute bottom of the lodging business was Rocket 88, a regional motel chain that had sputtered to some marginal distinction throughout Louisiana and Texas. They were known for their add campaign that bragged, 'We'll leave the TV on for you'. All of their rooms were decorated with various car parts including painted over rusty fender panels from the 50's and 60's. Sleeping soundly in room B - 15 was Gloria Spears, a young mother, and her eleven-year-old daughter, who had flown in the night before from Dallas.

At 8:00 AM the Rocket 88 replica telephone began ringing, and was answered by the slim lined lemon blonde mom with shocks of cascading split ends.

"Ginger, honey. Ginger, that was our wake up call. Drat it, Ginger, wake up!" called Gloria as she tried to lift her wrinkled face off of the pillow and roll her meager proportions out of the bed.

Ginger shook her brunette head, put her hands on the floor and began walking on her hands in order to get herself out of bed. The gangly rawboned pre teen slithered her way on to the floor, then rolled up into a big ball with her blanket and pillow.

"Honey, you get into the shower! You have to look even more beautiful today than usual," Gloria said to her daughter, who was at that awkward stage of looking like neither a child nor a teen. "When you get done with your shower I'll put on *Mr. Rogers* for you. I'm going to call grandma back in Dallas," she said, while shoving three sticks of gum into her mouth.

Gloria looked blankly at the adolescent toy that was their phone, then finally figured out that she would have to retract the convertible top to find the numbers for dialing.

"Mom, this is Gloria. Drat it mom; turn up the volume on your phone! This is Gloria."

Gloria listened to Grandma then responded, "It was too late to call last night. Of course I'm okay. We're staying at one of the better places in San Antonio. The only problem is that the TV never goes off. I had to pull the plug out of the wall."

The blonde mom listened again to her mom, then continued, "How is our room decorated? It's decorated in old bumpers and headlights from a 1958 Edsel."

She listened again. "Shush it mom, you are so tacky. Why is everything in Texas so tacky? I'd like to move somewhere with real refined people," she stated dramatically while smacking her gum with pugilistic delight.

"Mom, it's not really a contest. I'm sure that Ginger and I have already won. This going to Freshman Pharmaceuticals is just a formality."

She listened again, "Hush it mom, you really didn't send me to finishing school. You sat me down in front of *Mr. Rogers* and threatened me that I had better turn out like him. This is our big chance. We could get five thousand dollars towards Ginger's college fund."

Gloria paused. "Of course the salon is not going to fold because I took a day off. They have plenty of extras that will handle Chair # 12 for one day."

She paused. "We're going to wear our matching sailor outfits with the red sweaters, blue canvas purses and the white deck shoes."

"Yes, I know it's a little warm for those outfits, but they're our most striking outfits. And of course, they're sending a car around for us."

"Mother, zip it, there is nothing to worry about. I went on the Internet at work, and looked up this Freshman Pharmaceuticals. They're worth two billion dollars. And, I brought all of the documents. All that they do is interview me and Ginger. I've got to go. Ginger is done with her shower and it's almost time for *Mr. Rogers*."

Gloria got down on her hands and knees, her long hair dangling on the floor, and searched for the electrical plug behind the tin dresser with the authentic Oldsmobile decal. She put the plug back into the wall and turned on the TV as she was sucking on her gum and making a noise like a roller coaster in full descent. "I want you to be like him," she told her daughter. "Get dressed while I'm in the shower. We've got to catch the bus at ten o'clock so you need to help me out. We're wearing our sailor outfits like I told you. Put on your white deck shoes and don't keep changing shoes all the time."

After a steamy and sticky bus ride through the labyrinths of San Antonio, Gloria and her awkwardly angular beauty arrived at the Freshman Pharmaceutical's Corporate Headquarters. With their sailor suit costumes, Navy purses, and flaming red sweaters, they had been the only topic of conversation for all of the other public transport passengers who were mainly decked out in tattered cut off blue jeans, short shorts, tank tops and muscle shirts.

Looking like Waves on leave, Gloria and Ginger strode into the contest waiting room. Gloria took one fast glance around the room and declared to her daughter, in a forceful stage whisper, "Look at all of the losers, honey." It was without a doubt, a small but interesting collection of mothers and offspring, all dressed in matching outfits. Before the sailor girls had arrived, the waiting group of contestants had been evenly split genderwise, two-and-two. One mother and twelve-year-old son had on matching University of Texas football jerseys, even though her number was 99 and his was 9. This was an accurate reflection of their disparate sizes. The other mother and male clone were going for some kind of a trekkie look with their brown outfits, shoulder pads and gold medallions. The mothers and daughters had assuredly trumped the boys. The first mother/daughter combination that Gloria saw was dressed in prominent sartorium of the athletic variety. The mom and her eight-year old darling were wearing royal purple Spandex outfits with snapdragon shoes and lilac headbands. The other mother and her little princess, also about eight years old, were dressed in pink chiffon ballerina outfits.

The waiting room decor was based on mutant versions of the company's official colors, and obviously the product of a tragically deranged mind. On the walls were immense pictures of the company's products including heart valves, enema kits, and their new women's wonder drug, Bimbotol. The chairs were made to look like pills and the coffee tables like diaphragms. The receptionist's desk was made to look like a large bedpan and contained an extremely jolly jumboesque receptionist.

"Hi sweetie. I'm Gloria Spears and this is my daughter Ginger," said the sailor mom while crackling her gum. "We're here to sign up for that five thousand bucks."

"Hello, Gloria," answered the receptionist while jiggling all over and giggling to herself. "Did you bring all of your documentation?"

"Sure did sweetie."

"Gloria, I have a few documents for you to sign. This one says that you willingly participated in this contest without any outside coercion."

Gloria smacked her gum a couple of good whacks and said, "You mean other than the possibility of winning five thousand dollars toward my little starlets college fund."

"Oh yes, I suppose so," giggled the receptionist. "I don't really understand this stuff, I just have to ask you to sign it. This second one here, it says you've given us the right to interview you," she continued bubbling as the two young boys began playing catch with a football.

"Shattner, you be careful with that ball," calls out the trekkie mom.

"How bad is this interview that I have to sign for it?"

"Oh Gloria, you're so smart," chortled the receptionist as her bulbous jowls flapped in agreement. "You just feel free to ask me any question. I just don't have any answers. Now this one gives us consent to interview your daughter. This next form says that you give us informed consent to conduct a thorough physical examination."

"Wait! Sweetie! What do you mean physical exam?" Gloria replied, almost swallowing her gum.

"This form says that you give us informed consent to conduct a thorough physical exam."

"Look! Sweet cakes, ain't nobody here been informed of nothing. You mean all of these other bimbos here have consented to a physical exam? How do I know that it's a real doctor and not some pervert? So how many women are you going to pick?" All conversation in the waiting room had stopped. All eyes and ears were on Gloria as Shattner's mom performed a death grip on her laser light ray.

Even though she was getting that nervous jello look the receptionist continued on, "I'm not really at liberty to say, but I believe they are looking for three women."

"They are going to pick three out of the five of us?"

"I'm not really at liberty to shake that information with you, but, yes. And, Gloria, the last thing for you to sign is our contract, that says if selected you will be in Austin, at the designated time and place, on June 20, 1998."

"Give me those forms. I'll think about it."

Giving her daughter a subtle follow me wiggle of her finger, Gloria picked up the forms and headed directly toward the already anxious ballerina mom who appeared to be a personal friend of Dr. Vertigo.

"So did you sign all of those consent forms?"

"Yes, I think so," said the tutu mom.

"You're going to let some tacky San Antonio red neck look at all your parts?"

"I think so. It is five thousand dollars."

"So what bank did your daughter come from?"

"The After Glow Bank in Chicago, I think."

"Oh, how sad, how sad," Gloria feigned as she wrung her hands in phony desolation. "What a shame, that you wasted your time coming here today. My little starlet is from the Beverly Hills Bank. Walter Mathau, I believe," Gloria continued as she smirked at the shrinking mom with the spinning brain. "Those are such nice ballerina outfits. Last week at work, I was watching a show on cable about a mom and daughter that dressed in their little ballerina costumes. They would go down to the docks in Chicago and pick up longshoremen," Gloria finished just as a football came sailing by her ear and crashed into one of the lamps designed like a Foley catheter. The near miss with the football startled Gloria, and caused her to spit out her gum, making it a near lethal projectile that hit the trekkie mom in the face. The ball had been badly thrown by the football son and was now laying on the other end of the room next to the burnt ocher banner that read 'In Rush We Trust.'

Gloria whisked across the waiting room and grabbed the football. Taking a fingernail file from her purse, she decisively plunged it through the bladder of the football, which caused a vile ceremonious bang, startling everyone just as the ballerina mom and daughter tiptoed out the door.

"So I suppose you're going to let that red neck quack look at you," Gloria spewed at big number 99, as she handed her the deflated ball.

"I've got nothing to hide," number 99 spewed back.

"And lots of places to hide it," Gloria countered.

Big number 99 pulled herself out of her chartreuse pill chair to reveal that she was a full head taller than Gloria. "Now you prissy miss with the split ends, I could knock you across this here room," she started just as Shattner and his mom headed for the depressurized exit chamber.

"Beam me up Shattner, beam me up," mumbled the trekkie mom as she was transported out of the moss inspired mutant room.

"Okay Sweet cakes, now you've got three," Gloria said to the dumbfounded receptionist. "You ain't got no need to look at any of my parts. And you ain't got no need to look at all of sweet 99's parts either. Just give me the five grand! Care for a pack of gum? Let me sign that contract. See you in Austin on the twentieth."

Chapter Fourteen
May 13, 1998
Austin, Texas

It was an absolutely splendiferous day in the middle of May, which was not being enjoyed at all by KLRU's Sig Eros and Larry Tacoma. They were cloistered inside of their studio preparing for a rematch with Archbishop Nelson. Neither man nor mouse in any of the far reaches of the studio had missed hearing of Bishop Boom Boom's first visit. Even the bats in the belfry knew it was best to sleep when the Bishop was around. That afternoon was the most necessary of missions, as it was their last face-to-face meeting before June 20th.

The joke around the office was that the meeting should have been held in a bunker and not an office. They had arranged their desks, secured the sturdiest of chairs, and put all telephone calls on hold. At exactly 2:00 PM one holy steam rolling juggernaught hit their office.

"Mighty nice of you busy media execs to meet with me," said the Archbishop. "I hope you don't mind that I prepared the agenda for today's meeting," he said as he started his rapid-fire monologue. " First we fly into Bergstrom on the afternoon of the 20th. Pay attention! The Governor has arranged for the

National Guard to handle traffic. Second, the motorcade to the Andersen/Moore compound is arranged. All county officials are on board. Third, note all the details for the reception. Porter should attend. Are you boys following along? Fourth, the procession to the Governor's mansion. The city has their orders. Next, the Pope will freshen up and nap at the Mansion. Any questions? Sixth, the parade from the mansion to the studio. Seven, His Holiness arrives thirty minutes before show time and retreats to the room you set up for him. See the attached instructions. Are you following this? Eight, at the beginning of the show there will be a procession through the aisles. The Pope will stop and let a few of the faithful kiss his ring. Listen carefully! Next, he will receive a blessing at the altar. Number ten, The Word plays three songs. Eleven, His holiness says a fifty-minute High Mass. Twelfth, he delivers the unification speech. Thirteenth, he parades out through the aisles and greets more of the audience. Any little questions, before we discuss your list of responsibilities?" said the Archbishop, as he stopped machine gunning information at them.

"I have a point of clarification, not really a question," Sig began. "We really only have forty minutes for the Pope. I'd say your outline would take a minimum of ninety minutes."

"Then find me another fifty minutes."

"I don't know how to say this in Latin but we are at the very most a sixty minute show."

"Are you saying my eloquently outlined thirty page document is not workable?"

"In a word, yes. You can take over the state of Texas. You can reorganize Travis County. You can close down the city of Austin but you can't disrupt us. We're bigger than the state of Texas. We're television," said Sig.

"You hombres sound a little arrogant to me," Nelson replied as he puffed out his chest.

"Bishop, I don't think we should start using the A word," replied Larry hesitantly.

"Well, I know arrogance when I see it," said the Archbishop, as Larry rolled his eyes. "And little fellow you can refer to me as Archbishop," he continued. "So where did my twenty minutes go?"

"We have to promote our sponsors, and Porter made a deal to include the University of Texas Swing Band," said Sig.

"What an idiotic idea that is."

"Imagine a swing band on a music show," stated Larry as he pruned up his face.

"So where did Porter get that goofy idea?"

"Actually the Governor's daughter is part of the swing band. Not to mention, they are outstanding musicians and have won a case full of trophies," Sig replied. "Would you like to call the man who is arranging the National Guard for you and tell him that his daughter can't be on the show?"

"I see your point. That's a damn fine swing band and I'd bop anyone who said they weren't. Now, like I've tried to tell you boys, mature conversation and compromise is the only way to get things done."

"Archbishop, we like your thinking," said Larry.

"You realize that the Catholic/country unification speech is the Pope's main priority. But I tell you the Pope is in love with that Wisconsin band."

"Where did the Pope hear that band?" asked Larry.

"He never actually heard them."

"He loves them but he's never heard them?" asked Larry.

"He loves their name, The Word. You realize that symbolism is very big in the church. In the beginning was The Word. That's strong symbolism."

"Symbolism?" repeated Larry. "We're a country mu... never mind."

"Where did you first hear about this band?" asked Sig

"I have a network of intelligent, ah, intelligencia around the country. I knew they had the je ne sais quoi to uplift this blessed event."

"Have you ever heard *Brown Eyed Handsome Cow?*" asked Larry.

"No."

"It's about a cow wearing a brassier."

"That's Wisconsin for you. They'll do anything for their cows."

"It's a cross your heart bra for Chr... crying out loud," screeched Larry.

"Steady, little fellow. We'll have them sing some Christian songs. I have regular contact with this trio. Don't worry," said the Archbishop as he laid his huge paw on Larry's shoulder.

"What do you mean trio? They are a duo, aren't they Larry?" Asked Sig.

"They are a duo," confirmed Larry, wiggling around to get the Bishop's hand off of his shoulder.

"I found this group and I say they are a trio."

"You found them but you've never heard them."

"Gentlemen, I found them. Don't try and make my trio a duo."

"We're telling you what we know."

" I have made numerous concessions this afternoon. Now it's your turn. Just call Johnny Lee and ask him."

"Who's Johnny Lee?" asked Sig.

"He's the leader of my trio."

"Michael Vaughn is the leader of your duo," said Larry.

"Johnny Lee is a great Catholic. He bought the most Pagan Babies in Wisconsin and is the leader of my trio."

"Pagan Babies?" asked Larry in his squeaky voice with his nose almost touching his forehead.

"Johnny Lee is very important, very busy and he has cancer. This Vaughn is probably his leg man. What does it matter if it's a duo or a trio. That hillbilly stuff all sounds pretty appalling."

"Appalling?" asked Larry, with sky high modulation.

"Appealing, I meant appealing. Gentlemen, the Pope has decided that they are going to be at his altar on your show on June 20th. It wouldn't matter if one of them was a tuba player."

"A tuba player," squealed Larry.

"Gentlemen, I must remind you that you voluntarily took on this responsibility. We could have signed with the *Grand Ole Opry*. The world is watching you. Don't screw up."

"Pagan Babies, tuba players," repeated Larry.

"Gentlemen, pay attention! Your swing band can play before the Pope arrives on stage. When the Pope comes out there will be a short procession and blessing, followed by a leaner unification speech. Then a Saturday afternoon version of the mass, followed by songs from The Word. The Pope will quickly parade out. There are your forty minutes gentlemen!"

"Sounds almost workable," said Sig.

"Yes, see how much we can accomplish with cooperation."

"We have a couple of items to discuss," said Sig.

"I'm not done yet. On June 19th the Deacon from Rome, Texas will arrive. You will need a room for him and his garments. Show him around the studio and the altar. He'll be serving the Pope during the High Mass, ahem, the Saturday afternoon version of the mass."

"I thought you'd be doing that," said Sig.

"I'll be in the background. I shun the spotlight, myself."

"Here are the items we need to discuss with you," Sig said in a deeper, louder voice.

Archbishop Nelson continued, with no regard for Sig's bass attempt, "You'll need to have a processional crucifix, an incensor, holy water dispenser, and four altar boys complete with cassocks. I've already talked to Father Zamboni and he'll work with you. Also on the 19th our printer will deliver gold embossed pamphlets for everyone in the audience. Are you still with me gentlemen? Here are the plans for building the altar."

"Wait," Sig shouted, in his damn it I've had enough voice. "We already have the altar under construction. We're the experts in putting on a television show."

"You execs only do country music shows. This is a Papal visit."

"What?" Larry squealed.

"We have it designed and under construction. Now we have some items to discuss," Sig continued with the sound of total exasperation.

"Of course gentlemen, I am always at your service."

"We're having some problems with our air exchanger. The incensing will have to be held to an absolute minimum," Sig continued.

"If you had held this outside in the amphitheater."

"There is no amphitheater!"

"The Pope was doubting your sincerity when I told him that."

"Our sincerity," Larry said hitting a high C.

"Sure, we can keep the incensing to a minimum."

"We need to have His Holiness conduct a blessing of the virgins," Sig continued.

"What do you mean a blessing of the virgins?" said the mammoth Archbishop as he bent forward and glowered at Sig, who was glowering back.

"We have some virgins in the audience and we need the Pope to bless them."

"How did they get into the audience?"

"They entered a contest."

"What kind of contest?"

"A Virgin Birth Contest."

The Archbishop bent even closer to Sig and said, "I've never heard of a Virgin Birth Contest. There was only one Virgin Birth. Are you trying to make a mockery out of this blessed event?"

"A mockery!" Larry intoned, working his face into a perfect pretzel. "A mockery? We have a country music show with a visiting Pope, a swing band, a dairylang twang tweeo, and some Virgin Marys. Why would you call that a mockery?"

"Let me explain. The contest was Porter's idea," Sig said.

"That should explain it," said Larry.

Sig started again, "Porter reckoned that with all of the artificial insemination going on, some of these women were technically virgins. And we got a half a million dollar contribution from Freshmen Pharmaceuticals to hold the contest."

"What does Freshman Pharmaceuticals make?"

"Bimbotol, it's a female enhancer."

"So Porter held a contest to promote Bimbotol in conjunction with His Holiness appearing on your show. That's outrageous."

"No it's show business. It got us a lot of free publicity. I'm surprised you didn't hear about it," Sig replied.

"I don't watch that kind of TV"

"We've chosen three women and promised them that the Pope would bless them," said Sig.

"We didn't like the idea either," said Larry with semi-composure. "Virgins have no place in country music. I mean, contests have no place on a country music show."

"The Pope is not going to like this. We'll call them special women, yes, special women of the church. That's how you refer to them from now on!"

Sig and Larry nodded in agreement.

"I suppose it's too much to ask that these special women are married?"

"No, I think they'll be in the audience praying for husbands."

"That's what I figured."

"Last time you were here we didn't get to show you the studio. Would you like to see the studio now?"

"No, I trust you gentlemen implicitly. I'm sure there's a studio." The Archbishop stood up and got louder, "I'll be here on the 19th to meet with Johnny Lee and his trio. I'll inspect the studio then."

Out burst Bishop Boom Boom as Sig vigorously shook his pale head, and Larry grabbed his cheeks and stretched them several feet from his face.

Chapter Fifteen
June 18, 1998
Austin, Texas

What a thrill it was for a small town banker chick to fly to Dixie. I thought that our pilot looked like Leslie Nielsen but, of course, Davie said I'd been watching too many reruns of *Airplane*. I have to tell you, with all of the fuss about the Pope coming to America all of the newspapers and magazines were running every sort of related article. On our flight to Austin I was reading the June issue of Women Unlimited which is targeted more toward the bi-coastal babes than we Midwestern women. They had an article about the creation of the world, claiming it was based on new evidence that God was a woman. I'm pretty traditional so I don't know if I buy God being a woman or not, but it made good reading. And maybe God creating the world in a month instead of a week is something I should consider, if I really want to expand my mind.

The article said that God worked on creation in conjunction with her moods. She created whatever suited her that day. During the first week she felt calm, kindhearted and benevolent, and she created many of our beautiful and exotic creatures. She created Hawaii, the Bahamas, and the Caribbean, and surrounded them with coral reefs and vibrant tropical fish.

That first week with endless exuberance, she created the songbirds, butterflies, orchids, house plants, and peacocks. As that week went on nothing seemed out of sight as she created the stars, the moon, milking cows and Santa's reindeer.

As the week ended, her mood changed and she became more adventurous and vigorous creating the panthers, lions and jaguars to prowl the jungles, eagles and cranes to dominate the skies, plus gold and diamonds to dazzle humans. She had one of those days where she felt the prankster and thought it fun to pull our leg. She made the giraffes, rhinoceros, pelicans and parrots. Another day she felt particularly benevolent to men and created hops, barley and cannabis, plus fetching them thousands of mongrel dogs.

Then she began cramping and bloating, and her mood turned bitter. She dumped tons of salt into the ocean and gave the dogs fleas. She created termites, vultures and vipers. She grew prickly pear, bladderwart, and sauerkraut. She devised hurricanes, tornadoes and zirconium. She sand blasted the Mojave and Sahara Deserts. Then she stopped to bitch at the angels or things could have been worse. God felt faint exhaustion after such a pugnacious and productive week, therefore the next week she worked on little things like fungi, algae and lice.

The last week, she was in an undetermined mood, and not sure what she wanted. She planned the eclipse. She removed half of the monuments from monument valley, then put them back again. She couldn't decide on a color for the zebras. And she finished by creating crowberry, kelp, and house cats. That was one powerful article and sure gave me a lot to think about. Well, except for the fact that as I finished the article we touched down in Austin.

Our luggage, complete with Davie's herbal tea, arrived at the same airport and at the same time as we did.

Roy had found us the historical Austin Motel for our abode away from home. In it's hay day the Austin had been a stage coach stop along the fabled Golden Corridor. As the city of Austin grew in other directions the neighborhood suffered and this once proud stage stop became a warehouse. It seemed that the city forgot about this area and it became populated by drug dealers and those, you know, lady of the evening types. Fortunately for us the Austin Motel and the rest of this entire area was renovated about ten years ago. It was affordable and within easy walking distance of KLRU. Roy pronounced it, "Better looking than a bratwurst drenched in sauerkraut." I was sure the preppie eighteen-year-old at the desk had no idea what he was talking about.

After checking in, we found more of the motel's charm. All of their rooms were done in different themes. Davie and I had a room that was done in a frontier motif. The headboard was an old wagon wheel and there were pictures of grubby looking cowboys from the early days of Austin. Roy and Michael had a tropical room that was done in pastels with flamingos everywhere. The sign in front said it all: 'So close, yet so far out'. After unpacking we congregated in Roy's room, listened to him tell the most outrageous stories and waited for Johnny Lee Linton.

After a couple of hours reliving the mud wrestling contest and other notable events, Johnny Lee showed up. He probably wondered why we were all so teary eyed. Well, Johnny Lee had sure grown up to be something to look at all right. I knew immediately that the buffers had been working all morning to polish this copper toned idol. Even carrying a garment bag, he made a dignified entrance and extended his hand like a true Southern gentleman.

"Howdy," Davie said, trying to be Texan. "It's been a long time. This is my gurl friend Marion Hensley and you remember my pardner, Michael Vaughn. And this is our roadie, Roy Ryman."

"I'm not really anybody's roadie," Roy exclaimed. "I own a nightclub in Green Bay. After Michael begged me to be their roadie, I said sure, I'd help them out."

"Pleased to meet you Mister Roy. I'm part owner in a nightclub myself. We'll have to talk."

This was already getting good. I'd heard The Howling Dog called a lot of things but never a nightclub. I sure got a funny feeling when that Johnny Lee shook my hand and looked at me.

"Are you related to Stevie Ray Vaughn?" Johnny asked Michael in a southern drawl that showed he was already condescending to his simple country cousins.

"No."

"Do you know they have a statue of Stevie Ray here in Austin?" asked Johnny.

"I didn't know that. Maybe we are related."

"They're talking about erecting my statue in Green Bay," said Roy.

Davie and Michael burst out in a big laugh. I could sense that Roy was already developing a little attitude toward Johnny. That was not good. Michael and Davie were ready to bathe him in blarney and polish his apples all the way back to Atlanta. If Johnny Lee didn't go along with them, it was going to be painful for everyone. The boys needed to find out how well Johnny knew the Archbishop. Roy's statue comment did ease the tension a bit and we all sat down on the fluorescent pink flamingo lounge chairs.

"How did you find this mausoleum?" asked Arrogant Atlanta.

"I found it," snapped Roy causing a little flinch across Johnny's face.

"My tastes run a little more uptown. I'm staying at the Kingland Resort on Lake LBJ, five hundred a night and well worth it." Johnny uptown replied.

I quickly touched Roy's arm and gave him as much of a smile as I could. The wordy red head swallowed whatever words he had readied for Johnny, as all of the guys were looking my direction. Wanting to give Johnny a big cheese head welcome, I started in a soothing tone, "Johnny, my man Davie has talked about nothing but how incredible it was going to be to see you again."

"Incredible," Roy repeated under his breath.

"I remember you from your Green Bay days. You look about the same," said Davie.

"I remember you, too, from the Riverside Ballroom. What in the name of Robert E. Lee happened to you?"

"I guess I didn't age as well as others," said Davie. "But we sure showed you a thing or two at the Riverside. You left town shortly after that."

"My leaving town had nothing to do with the Riverside. And I'd say I was twice as good as you Buzzards," Johnny responded as each word dripped with syrupy self-satisfaction.

"Johnny let's call it a draw," Michael added quickly, knowing that Davie still had a raw nerve over the Riverside incident. "You can live with that, right Davie?"

"Davie has cancer," added Roy quickly.

"Sorry to hear that, Davie."

"I'm on chemotherapy, which should buy me a few more months. I really feel fit as a fiddle right now. Well, an old fiddle."

"He's on the best pain medicine known to man," Roy added.

"Oh, what's that?" asked Johnny.

"What do you do?" asked Michael, as he shot Roy a look and quickly jumped in to change the course of the conversation.

"I'm mainly a piano player at my night club and a few other clubs. I do some TV commercials for a couple of Georgia based businesses. I have a half-hour radio show where I play the piano and tell stories about the musical history of the area. And I still find time to perform one piano mass a week. I really pack 'em in too. Makes me feel so close to God. Davie, I will pray for you," said Johnny Lee puffing up like a bloated carp.

"They must have closed up the entire town just so you could come here," said Roy.

"It's costing me a thousand dollars a day to be here."

"Johnny we're thrilled to have you here and it's worth a thousand dollars just to meet you," said Michael.

"And maybe more when we hear about how well you know the Archbishop," added Davie.

"Actually he was Bishop Nelson then," Johnny said.

"Bishop, Archbishop. Where was he living?" asked Michael.

"He was living in Chicago, however, according to Sister Lynn he was traveling a lot because of the Pagan Babies."

"Did he travel to Green Bay?" asked Davie.

"Oh yes, many times. He was very interested in meeting benevolent Catholics like myself who had sacrificed so much to save so many pagans."

"How often did you meet the Archbishop," asked Michael

"Bishop!"

"Yes, how often did you meet the Bishop?"

"Well that's an interesting story."

"Oh Johnny, we'd be so interested in your story," I added as Davie gave me a sly look of approval.

"I had bought over a hundred Pagan Babies."

"A hundred Pagan Babies!" Roy interrupted.

"Johnny, please continue," I said. However, I doubt that he really heard Roy as he was absolutely self absorbed by then.

"On the day that the Bishop was in town I was playing in the school orchestra."

"Did you meet him?" Davie asked.

"I'll tell you all about it. Sister Lynn brought him to the high school so we could meet. I was so honored that he stood in the back and listened to the entire concert."

"And after the concert?"

The Bishop and Sister Mary Lynn waved to me from the back of the hall. She said he was in a hurry to return to Chicago."

"Ohhh! And that was your only meeting with the Archbishop?"

"Yes, what a wonderful man."

That news joyfully eased our tension. The Archbishop wouldn't recognize him from that brief encounter. It seemed to me that Johnny wanted to talk more about those Pagan Babies. The boys wanted to chit chat a little more before hitting Johnny with the big news. None of us knew what Roy was thinking.

"How long did you live in Green Bay?" Michael asked.

"Four years. The four longest years of my life."

"So you don't like Green Bay?" Roy asked in his contentious manner.

"I think of it as being completely north of the civilized world."

"Roy was ready to respond, but Michael beat him to it. "So, what do you think of Austin?"

"Naturally, I did some research on the city before I came here. Did you do any research?" asked Johnny with a tone that said he was sure his country cousins had not.

"I found this motel that's just four blocks from the studio," Roy retaliated.

"Then Mister Roy, you must know that this motel sits in the heart of the drug and prostitution area," said Johnny, who seemed to be holding his own with the verbose mister Ryman.

"Not drugs!" said Davie with mock horror as he went to his suitcase and pulled out his box of herbal tea.

"Well mister Johnny Lee, for your information, this area has been rehabilitated," Roy replied.

"Rehabilitation!" said Davie, as he swayed to some imaginary music and rolled himself a joint.

"What are you rolling?" asked Johnny.

"A cigarette."

At that point I was thinking that if it wasn't for Michael, we might just as well have gotten on the next plane and flown home. He tried again, "So what did your research tell you about Austin?"

"I know the population and the major industries. What do you think the number one tourist attraction is?"

"I'm sure it will be *Austin City Limits* after we get done playing there," boasted Davie, as he exhaled vigorously in Johnny's direction.

"Wrong. It's bat watching. There are two million bats in Austin," said Johnny Lee as he got a strong sweet whiff of woe when he realized that Davie was smoking pot.

"I always imagined that the Holy Ghost was like an albino bat," said a more tranquil Davie.

"You may then get your wish to see the Holy Ghost, as your motel is just a block from Bat Bridge," said Johnny Lee.

"Bats eat mosquitoes," added Roy, "but then I suppose you don't have mosquitoes in Atlanta."

"You know Johnny, we really love Atlanta," started Davie. Yes, Michael and I headed out for Atlanta once but we stopped in Nashville on the way. Well, we ended up in some sticky business in the old Music City and never got to Atlanta."

Roy was right; Davie could sure fake sincerity with the help of a little weed.

"All I know is that you stole the Braves," added Roy.

"That was forty years ago."

"I'm still mad about it."

"He's not really mad, just nostalgic," Michael tried as he rolled his eyes and looked at me.

Roy was getting over heated. Johnny continued overbearing, and Davie was becoming over medicated.

"And another fact you fellows should know is that the KLRU studios were once closed down by the Austin City Fire Marshall. We're going to be performing in a tinderbox. That place could go up in flames at any time."

"I don't think we can do anything about that now," said Michael. "There are a couple of other details we need to discuss about our performance."

"Good, I brought some outfits for you to wear," said Johnny as he went to the clothing bag he had carried in. He took out a couple of glitzy black satin suits. The coats had wide lapels and a half dozen silver sequined stars. The matching pants had silver sequined stripes down the legs. The sparkling silver suits were to be worn with a white silk shirt that had bilious ruffles down the front.

"So this is what the pimps wear in Atlanta," Roy whispered to Davie.

Davie inhaled deeply. "Interesting," he said blowing out a huge plume of Maui Wowie.

"Actually we brought you an outfit to match ours," said Michael, as he grabbed a hat box off of the table. "Here's your hat," said Michael, as he handed Johnny a brown twelve-gallon hat.

Johnny coughed. Michael then showed him his western cut brown denim suit. The pants and jacket were covered with leather fringe. As he looked at the denim suits, Johnny was losing his tan.

"Let's take the outfits over to KLRU tomorrow and let them decide," said Johnny. I imagined he felt he had a better chance with the studio than Michael and Davie.

"I think you should decide today," said Roy.

"No, Johnny's right. Let's let the studio decide," said Michael.

"Anyway Roy, by tomorrow, Michael and I may be taking a real liking to those black satin suits," said Davie as he grinned at Roy.

"Mighty mature of you Wisconsin boys," said Johnny. "By the way how much are we being paid for this gig?"

"Da money," exhaled Davie and looked toward Michael.

"The money is really secondary. We're here to help out Sister Mary Lynn and the Archbishop."

"How secondary?"

"Didn't you call Sister Lynn begging to see the Pope? And didn't she arrange it for you? You weren't talking money then."

"I called her for the Archbishop's phone number. When he heard about me he immediately wanted to help. I guess out of gratitude for all those Pagan Babies."

"Begging the sister. That's what we heard," said Davie in sing song fashion.

"Union scale. We're being paid union scale," said Michael.

"I can't work for union scale."

"You're doing this to meet the Pope. And *Austin City Limits* only pays union scale."

"Okay. I can work for union scale, but of course they will flash our names and 800 numbers on the screen during the close ups, won't they?"

"Wow, that might be confusing," said Davie, as he stared into the tropical sunset on the ceiling.

"What Davie means is that we're dealing with public television, and we just hope their cameras can do close ups,"

"I've brought the music for the songs we should work on. Does this antiquarian establishment have a piano I can use?"

"You won't exactly need a piano, " said Davie, trying to stifle a little chuckle.

"Of course I need a piano, I'm not a tuba player."

"Davie is right. We don't need a piano player," said Michael.

"Sister Lynn said we were going to perform. When I perform, I play the piano."

"She said you would perform. Did she mention the piano? asked Michael.

"No, no, no she didn't," sang out Davie.

"I promised Sister Lynn that I would do everything I could to help ya'll, but you cheese heads are making this very difficult."

"Now, now, Sister contacted us before you contacted her," Davie added.

"She told me that you contacted her," Johnny said.

"Why are you dragging the reputation of this saintly nun into this, especially when she is not here to defend herself? You should be ashamed, calling one of the purest women in Green Bay a liar," said Davie with total sincerity, compliments of Mary Jane.

"If anybody is a liar, you are," Johnny retaliated.

"I hope you Brave stealing sympathizer aren't calling my friend a liar," inserted Roy.

I quickly saw the need for a woman's gentle hand in their macho discussion. I quickly popped myself out of the chair and wrapped my hand around Roy's mouth. "Now Gentlemen, you have the opportunity of a life time in front of you. My Davie is being a little over protective of his friend Sister Lynn," I continued as I left Roy and moved in front of Johnny. I looked Johnny Lee straight in the eye even though it gave me the eeriest of feelings. "And Johnny, you really meant to say that you're confused by them suggesting that you not play the piano. We understand what a great piano player you are." Johnny was still staring at me as I looked toward Davie who was mouthing to me, "I love you."

"We need you to play the tambourine," added Michael.

"Never! I'm the top piano player in Atlanta. I'm a celebrity, not an organ grinder's monkey."

"It's so good of you to consider it," I added with my best stage smile.

As I sat back down, I noticed Johnny's tan was fading even more rapidly.

"Johnny, the contract to perform is between *Austin City Limits* and our band. It's my signature on that document. We want you to join us, but we can do it with you or without you," stated Michael.

"No, you have to include me. I'm desperate to meet the Archbishop."

Then giving Johnny my most understanding look, rehearsed for years in the foreclosure department of the bank, I told him, "However, Johnny we are going to need you to make some other adjustments."

"What! I'm sorry Miss Marion, you are a very dynamic woman but they have rejected my outfits. They don't want to perform my music. And they say I can't play the piano. Now I can't think of any other compromise I could possibly make."

"Then just hold onto your satin britches," Roy whispered to Davie.

"Well pardner, I can," said Davie.

Michael jumped in without hesitation. "You see Johnny there was a little misunderstanding. The Archbishop thought that you were part of The Word. He actually got the impression that you are the bald part of The Word."

"No!" Johnny shouted as he came up out of his chair. "I'm not shaving my head. Are you guys totally nuts? It's that dope he's smoking," he cried out while pointing at my mellow minded cowboy.

"Johnny, Johnny," cooed Davie. "That's the beauty of it. You don't have to shave your head. Just let me borrow your name."

"No. Are you crazy? Then who do I become? I'm not becoming Davie Fender."

"That's perfect," said Davie smiling at no one in particular while Johnny eased himself back into his chair.

"What he means is that you have to take my name. I take Davie's name and he takes your name," explained Michael.

"Why?"

"Oh why baby why," sing songed Davie.

"I asked why?" demanded Johnny as he leaned forward toward Davie.

"Why what?" asked Davie.

"Why, why, why everything?" replied Johnny.

"Davie, I think it's your turn," I stated.

"Let me tell you the truth."

"You? The truth?"

Davie started telling Johnny about finding out that he had cancer and how depressed he had become. He paused. He told about his less than stellar life style and wanting to get a plenary indulgence from the Pope as he folded his hands and looked skyward. He regaled him with all of the details of *Austin City Limits* and Bobby Nelson. Johnny Lee's expression kept changing as Davie's story went on and on. I was sure that Johnny was pondering could any of this craziness be true? Davie mentioned how he met Sister Lynn and the phone call to the Archbishop that included discussion of the Pagan Babies. He explained that at the very end of her conversation Nelson remembered specifically who had sold the most Pagan Babies. Davie was masterful, and Johnny calmed considerably during the monologue. Johnny Lee hadn't come around completely but something in Davie's story had touched a chord with the Atlanta icon.

"So your saintly little nun didn't tell the whole truth," concluded Johnny.

"Johnny, sins are everywhere just waiting to happen," replied Davie.

"So what if I don't want to play along with your game of musical names?" asked Johnny.

"You said you were desperate to meet the Archbishop," Davie said.

"Johnny, if you're desperate to meet him we need your cooperation," said Michael.

"I didn't say desperate."

"You definitely said desperate!" stated Roy.

"Well, with all of this claptrap conversation whirling around here, I suppose I could have said anything."

"Johnny, the boys and I want to be your friends. We're sorry if some tiny little thing we said made you feel uncomfortable. I think we've just had some minor communication problems," I added.

"That's why I'm desperate to see the Archbishop. Communication problems. Honestly, I'm a great talent, but I'm very unhappy. Maybe I always was a little high strung. But you remember my dad, don't you? He was an absolutely gifted scientist, my idol, and the one that started me playing the piano. You probably heard the stories about him. Lies, they were all lies. Dad was the lead scientist for the Paper Company that developed four-ply toilet paper. A year later their main competitor came out with a similar four-ply product. Some of the Fort Harold executives believed that my father had sold out their technology. They accused him of industrial espionage and began criminal proceedings. That was why we left Green Bay in such a hurry. He spent ten years fighting the charges before he was finally cleared. By then he was a broken man. He was never the same and died a few years later. Every morning I have a vision of this frail desolate man that was my hero. And I am angry. But this anger has cost me dearly. My wife and I are on the outs more than the ins. My kids think I'm an old fossil and avoid me most of the time. Even my agent argues with me and I pay him good money to be subservient. I'm lonely. I want to talk to the Archbishop about those Pagan Babies, so I can find out who they are and where they live. I figure I saved them from paganism, they should be grateful. They would talk to me. They would like me. I have this big house. They could move right in. If I just had their phone numbers."

"Doesn't Atlanta have enough pagans already?" asked Roy, as the rest of us sat there temporarily amazed from Johnny's story about his father.

"No, pagans are from another country."

"Johnny, I hate to burst your bubble, but there are no Pagan Babies. You just gave money. Like the time I sponsored the Elsie Contest. It was just to make money."

"What kind of a night club do you have? Sponsoring an Elsie Contest."

"It was National Dairy Week. But the point is there are no pagans for you to call," Roy added.

"I don't believe that, Roy. I don't believe that at all, but Davie you can count me in. I think ya'll are nuts, but count me in on whatever con is going down."

Johnny was very surprised when Davie jumped out of his chair, gave him a big hug and added, "Johnny, I had no idea all of those things happened to your father. I'm sorry, very sorry for you," Davie finished and finally released hold of the breathless icon.

"That's great," said Michael. We're all in this together."

"Hold on a minute. You Greenlanders have missed the obvious," said Johnny. "We can just tell the truth," he continued, causing a momentary silence.

"Now I see why you can't get along with your wife," Roy said.

"Our contract, I mean your contract is with *Austin City Limits*. The Archbishop can't invalidate that. By the time we meet with him there'll be only twenty four hours until show time."

"Maybe he's on to something," said Michael.

"Pagan phone numbers, remember those pagan phone numbers," said Roy.

"Did we forget about Sister Mary Lynn?" asked Davie. "That sainted nun who fibbed and schemed and manipulated to get us all here. Her reputation is on the line. We need to protect her."

"Davie, you're the one trying to go to Heaven. I would think that you would want to tell the truth," concluded Michael.

"We must be loyal to Sister Lynn," I added.

"At this point it's really no longer a lie," Davie said. "The Archbishop is expecting the real Johnny Lee to have cancer. That's me, I get one point. He's expecting to meet the leader of The Word. That's not me, but it's also not him either. I get a half point for being a member of The Word. His name happens to be Johnny Lee. I'll give him one point for that. I win one and a half to one."

"And just what school of Logic did you graduate from?" asked Michael.

"Once everybody believes a lie it becomes the truth," Davie replied.

"He's right," said Roy. It's just like wrestling on TV. Everybody knows it's fake but we're honor bound to play along."

"Let's vote," said Michael.

"Do I get a vote?" asked Roy.

"Why? You're not going to be anybody. You're just going to be Roy," Michael reasoned.

"Liars vote, liars vote," chanted the obviously stressed out Johnny Lee.

"Imagine that, I'll be the most honest person at this gathering," said Roy.

"I vote to tell the truth," said Michael.

"I vote that we do the honorable thing and change names," said Davie.

"So Johnny it's up to you," said Michael.

"Don't worry about Sister Lynn and her reputation. Just do the right thing," I reminded.

"I have to vote with my friend Davie," said a beaming Johnny who had found old acquaintances that wanted him, overbearing and all. "I don't think that changing the truth now is part of God's plan. If I'm going to be Michael Vaughn then I'm going to have my picture taken in front of my cousin's statue."

Chapter Sixteen
June 19, 1998
Austin, Texas

Remember how Roy was begging to come along on the trip? At 6:00AM on June 19th the proverbial tiger turned and bit Roy in the tail, so to speak. *Austin City Limits* called the motel saying if Michael and Davie were going to perform then their roadie, one Mr. Ryman, needed to show up at the studio and get to work. Sometimes when your friends suffer it is so funny. Roy doesn't do mornings and oodles of people in Green Bay would swear he doesn't work. He agreed to show up at 10:00AM then flopped dead asleep for another three hours. Actually, this gave Roy some place to go while Johnny Lee and the boys met with the Archbishop. I decided that I'd had enough fun the day before and was going to do some shopping along nearby South Congress Avenue during the Archbishop's visit. Davie promised he was not going to smoke while Nelson was there. He hinted that he might even throw away the rest of his stash. We knew from Sister Lynn that the Archbishop had only an hour to meet with Johnny Lee and his band. This meant that the boys would have to tap dance around the truth for a mere sixty minutes.

The real repolished Johnny Lee arrived at Roy and Michael's room an hour before Nelson was due to arrive. He looked dapper and said that he had slept wonderfully in his five hundred dollar bed. Roy had already departed for his work assignment. I excused myself, clicked my heels, and headed out shopping. The three boys started chewing the fat like they were all cherished chums from Green Bay.

There was a boom boom boom on the door.

"That would be the Archbishop," said the real Michael. "I recognize the style."

As Davie made his way to the door it flew open and in burst the Archbishop. Our hero was so shocked that he almost forgot that he was now Johnny Lee.

"Howdy, I'm... I'm ...I'm pleased to meet you," Davie stammered.

"Of course you're Johnny Lee. I recognize the hair cut," said Nelson, pointing to Davie's bald head.

"I am, of course I am."

"Have you thought about Locks for Love?" asked the Archbishop, referring to the charity that provides wigs for cancer victims.

"No, I have a girlfriend. I mean a wife," Davie said, being not that sure of himself.

"You seem confused. Introduce me to these other men," Nelson demands. "I've heard of Michael Vaughn."

Confused is right, Davie thought to himself. I've got a fifty fifty chance to get this next part right.

"This is Michael Vaughn," Davie said, pointing to Johnny Lee.

The Archbishop grabbed his hand. "Are you related to Stevie Ray Vaughn?"

"Not me," replied the real Johnny Lee.

"And this is Da-Davie Fender," Davie said hesitantly and pointed to Michael.

"My God! You're not the annulment Fender are you?"

"Yes," replied the new Davie.

"No," replied the real Davie.

"You boys sure are confused. What is going on here?" the Archbishop demanded as only he could.

Michael gave Davie a hard glance, and started to explain, "Being Davie Fender, I'll answer the question. I am the manager Fender. That was your question, right?"

Nelson said, "No," opening his mouth very wide, "I asked if you were the annulment Fender," he continued as if talking to a deaf person.

"Oh, you said annulment," replied Michael, "no, that's my cousin Freddie."

"How many managers do you have? Those City Limitless dudes told me that you were the manager," the Archbishop ordered, pointing a finger at the real Johnny Lee.

Johnny swallowed hard. "Actually I'm not."

"Let me explain," said the real Michael.

"No, let me explain," interrupts the new Michael.

"Wait, what are you going to explain?" asked the real Davie, showing obvious tension.

"What the hell is going on?" asked the Archbishop.

"Nothing, nothing, nothing," sang out the three musicians in harmony.

"This is our leader," said the real Michael, putting his hand on Davie's shoulder.

Johnny Lee put his hand on the new Johnny Lee's other should and said, "Yes, this is the man." He then squeezed the cervical nerve in Davie's shoulder.

"Ow."

"There gentlemen, was that so hard? You sure do look familiar," said the Archbishop, looking at the real Johnny Lee.

"You've probably seen me on TV. I have a show down in At, Aa, A."

"Ashwaubenon," said the real Michael.

"What is Ashwaubenon?"

"It's a Green Bay suburb. It's the cultural center of the metroplex," the new bald Johnny Lee replied. "Yes the old city has grown a lot since we met at that high school pep rally."

"Concert!" interjected the real Johnny Lee.

"Yes, we met at the concert. I had so much pep back then that everything seemed like a pep rally."

"You sure have a strange Wisconsin accent," Nelson tried again with the real Johnny Lee.

"It's an Ashwaubenon accent," the real Michael piped in.

"Tell me, how did you all get together as a trio?" asked the Archbishop.

"It's a long story," said the real Davie, trying to buy some time.

"Long and interesting," added Michael, the new Davie.

"I'm sure that The Man can tell us," said the Archbishop in his social voice with the demanding tone.

"Well… We've all known each other forever," said Davie, the new Johnny Lee.

"That was sure a long interesting story," said the puzzled pontiff.

The conversation with the Archbishop seemed to be swirling in all directions and going nowhere. However, that may have been better than what happened next. I had finished up my shopping trip and assumed that the hour with Archbishop Nelson was long past. Wrong. I knocked on Roy and Michael's door causing a huge pause, as they were so engrossed in their deception. They looked at each other trying to figure out who would be the natural one to answer the door.

"Would somebody get the damn door," said Bishop Boom Boom.

Finally Davie jumped up and said, "I'm The Man," and opened the door. I gave him a big hug until I saw that the massive holy man was still there.

"How dare you," I said and pushed him aside, walking directly to Michael.

"Hello dear," he said, as I gave him a hug.

"Who are you?" Interrogated the holy man.

"I'm Marion, Davie's girl friend."

"Do you hug everyone?" he continued very pointedly.

I was a little flustered, and thought he wanted a hug. "Sure," I said and walked toward him.

"No! I don't want a hug."

"I'm sorry, was my arrival untimely? I could come back later," I tried. The atmosphere in the room was worse than a board meeting at the Cheese Head National Bank.

"Actually young lady, I must conclude my business here. But first of all, I want to congratulate The Word, especially Johnny Lee, for their contributions to The Church," said the Archbishop as he put a huge hand on Davie's shoulder. The same one that Johnny Lee had just tweaked.

"Thank you," said the new Johnny Lee, as he cringed from his cervical nerve that still tingled.

"Young lady, I don't know why you were hugging this man, but I should hug him too. However, I'm Bobby Nelson and I don't hug people. He's a devil of a piano player and he's a great friend to pagans," concluded the Archbishop, as he put both hands on Davie's shoulders and looked him straight in the eye.

"So where are all of those pagans?" asked the real Johnny Lee.

"You fellows aren't worried about a few pagans, are you?" Nelson said to the real Davie.

"Sometimes it crosses our minds," Johnny replied.

"Not now," Michael said firmly as he moved himself in slowly next to Johnny Lee and subtly put his hand on his shoulder.

"Now Dearie, I mean dear me, it's almost time for the Archbishop to go," I tried.

"We want their names and phone numbers," Johnny Lee persisted.

"Oh, look how late it is," Michael added

"I'm so sorry that you have to leave," I said again to the Archbishop, and went toward the door.

By this time Davie had gotten on one side of Johnny and Michael on the other and they were trying to walk him away from Nelson.

"I am really sorry you have to leave," I said in my best banker voice as I opened the door.

"Names and phone numbers," Johnny squawked, as the boys pinched him between them.

"I am really, really sorry you have to leave," I continued as Roy popped into the room.

"Now who is this?" demanded the Archbishop.

"Roy Ryman," they all shouted in unison.

"This is the one and only Roy Ryman," Michael said.

"Yes, that really is Roy," Johnny gushed.

"The real Roy Ryman," Davie bubbled over.

"Why all of this gushing and bubbling over Roy Rogers?" asked the Bishop.

"I've got something to tell you," Roy said.

"Not now Roy," said Michael. "The Archbishop was just leaving."

"I'll just walk out with him and get those phone numbers."

"I know you'll want to hear this," Roy repeated.

"Thank you for coming," Davie said to the Archbishop. "It was so good to see you again after all of these years. You look just the same."

"This is important," Roy tried again.

"Yes, like those phone numbers."

"I am really, really, really sorry you have to leave," I attempted while holding the door.

"Stop, all of you! Stop!" commanded the Archbishop. "Young lady close that door. Sit down!"

We all plopped into chairs as if our legs had been cut from under us.

"I know exactly what is going on here. And there are going to be some changes," boomed the Archbishop as our hopes and faces fell to the floor. "I have just come from *Austin City Limits*, and they have fouled up almost every assignment I gave them. The Deacon from Rome, Texas is a Deaconess. The Catholic Church has not had a Deaconess in a thousand years. I have no idea how I'm going to tell the Pope. Two of the special women were so special that they have canceled their appearance. And those media clowns failed to find any altar boys. We have thirty minutes more program than we have time. Therefore we have to make some changes. You gentlemen are no longer The Word. You are altar boys. And you, the hugging lady, are going to be one of the special women."

Chapter Seventeen
June 20, 1998
Austin, Texas

The tang of chili peppers perfumed the air as the four of us met for breakfast. El Sol, the motel's Tex Mex restaurant, was such a local favorite we were happy to be shoehorned into a corner booth. It was just like getting together after hours at The Howling Dog as we dined on huevos rancheros and listened to Roy tell about his experiences at Austin City Limits. But truthfully, I don't think this Green Bay girl could ever get used to having refried beans for breakfast.

Roy was explaining to us that after only two days on the job he was the second in command to the stage manager. This meant he was handling any details that the stage manager didn't want to mess with. He was put in charge of arranging the cubby holes that were being designated as dressing rooms. There was the last minute reconstruction of the altar. He was so proud, because most of the time he had a gaggle of college student volunteers following him around, hanging on his every word. All of them.

It was such a nonchalant start to such an important day. Any additional preparation by The Word had been nixed by the Archbishop. Only one of us really had anything to do until that afternoon. After breakfast roadie Roy had to hustle back to the studio. Michael and Johnny Lee headed over to see their cousin's statue. That left Davie and I with a couple of hours to walk through the historic University of Texas campus and its massive Red River brick buildings. I was holding tightly to his arm, like one of those dizzy co-eds, as we ambled under the towering Live Oaks splendidly shrouded in Spanish Moss. I could not have been more proud of my man. But the impact of meeting the Pope was beginning to get to Davie. Why, he had never even met a bishop before yesterday. Try as I might, he was getting more and more anxious.

"Marion, I really believe I must stop smoking pot," he said.

"Why is that?"

"It's illegal."

"Isn't it legal for pain control?" I asked.

"Not in Wisconsin. Only booze is legal."

"What about Texas."

"In Texas, you bite on a bullet," Davie responded.

"That's a law of man not a law of God's. He created marijuana and he created fire. Thousands of years ago, the Babylonians honored God by smoking marijuana. So why can't you honor God by smoking?"

"I don't know Marion. You're starting to think like Roy."

"Man created the automobile and highways. We kill hundreds of people on the highways every year. Marijuana is not that bad."

"I know you're right, but meeting the Pope is making me feel guilty."

I wasn't sure at the time who had convinced whom, but I continued to squeeze his arm tightly as we ambled past the expansive alabaster stone Lyndon Baines Johnson Library. I just wanted my man to be happy.

Later That Day

Bergstrom International Airport in Austin was at full attention for the arrival of the Pope. The tarmac was packed with fifteen glistening pearl white Rolls Royces, and Archbishop Nelson. His Holiness' jet swooped from the sky and delivered the Pontiff to the mass of admirers. As the motorcade wound through the Live Oaks of Austin, His Excellency stood under his glass bubble top and waved to the throngs. Cardinal Westwood had orchestrated a full seven-course pot luck dinner, complete with the countenance of country music, at the Moore Anderson Compound. At the Compound bountiful bevies of bourgeois bankers allied with befuddled Baptists blessed the Pontiff for bestowing a breath of bloom on their bucolic Bohemia. He was bushed. Before illuminating the information generation of America, the Pope would pause for a nap.

That Same Day at Austin City Limits

Let me pick up my story after once again being interrupted. I was thrilled to have been appointed a special woman. It meant that I got a good seat in the second row and didn't have to watch from the wings as planned. We had Gloria Spears, one of the original special women, Sig's wife, Fran, and myself all hoping to look very special for all of America.

The three guys and I arrived together at KLRU studios, and started looking for our weary roadie Roy. Within a few minutes we located the giddy looking redhead next to the stage, with his troupe of volunteers.

"It's good to see you hombres. Maybe I can get you into the dressing rooms before you run into Sig or Larry," Roy said. "Michael, I gave you three the biggest dressing room. Marion, I've got you in with the Deaconess in the next best dressing room."

"So where did you put the Pope?" I asked.

"He's not a native. He'll never know that I gave him the small dressing room."

Sig Eros' voice could be heard in the distance.

Roy motioned to one of his helpers. "Take this lady down to the Deaconess' dressing room."

I left with one of the student volunteers as I heard Sig calling, "Ron, roadie Ron."

"I think he means you," Johnny Lee piped up.

"Probably does," Roy replied. "You guys have got to get a load of this Deaconess. She's like a blonde Angel and a Deaconess all rolled into one."

"Rob, roadie Rob," Sig called out again.

"I better get you guys to your dressing room."

"Wait, you roadie, who is that with you?" Sig called from across the stage.

"These are the altar boys," Roy said as Sig approached.

"I'm Sig Eros. Which one of you is Michael Vaughn?"

"Wait Sig, where is Archbishop Nelson?" Roy asked.

"What does that matter? He's not coming until the Pope does."

"In that case, I'm Michael Vaughn," said Michael. "This is Davie Fender and Johnny Lee Linton," he continued, identifying the real men.

"I'm sorry about the change in plans," Sig added.

"We're still getting paid, aren't we?" asked Johnny. "I'm not getting to meet any Pagan Babies."

"I'll have my wife introduce you to Gloria, one of the special women. She may be pagan enough for you," said Sig. "You're Johnny Lee?"

"Yes."

"I thought the Archbishop said that you were the bald one," Sig said, causing a very pregnant pause.

"Do you find that Archbishop a little bit pushy?" asked Michael.

"Yes, we've had our moments."

"I've got to get these men to their dressing room," said Roy.

"Okay, remember Rod, we're going to have a run through before the Pope gets here," said Sig as he walked away.

"It's Roy!"

"Sure, Roy."

"Ha, I thought he was going to stick his nose into the dressing room assignments," Roy said.

Roy led the way for The Word to their plywood dressing room. Their instruments were in the corner of the hastily constructed cubicle, but they knew that they wouldn't be needing them. They milled around the room in search of their new identities.

"It's been a long time since I wore one of these," Johnny commented, as he held up one of the ruby red cassocks.

"Sig doesn't want you lighting this incensor," said Roy as he picked it up from amongst the crucifix and holy water dispenser. "It's something about the fire codes for the city."

"I used to be able to make those baskets really burn," said Johnny Lee with characteristic modesty, holding the incensor fondly in his hands.

"Before I leave, let me tell you something," said Roy. "I've arranged for you rising stars to get increased television time."

"Great idea roadie," said Johnny. "I was telling Michael this morning about some tricks we might try to make the most of this."

"How did you get us increased camera time?" asked Michael.

"I paid off the cameramen."

"What did you do," asked Michael, "bribe them with free admission to mud wrestling at The Howling Dog Saloon?"

"What is The Howling Dog Saloon?" asked Johnny

"That's the name of my night club," answered Roy.

"Doesn't sound like the name of a night club to me," replied Johnny. "And you hold mud wrestling along with the Elsie contests at your night club?"

"Not all the time," Roy answered; having his honcho status very temporarily dimmed. "Remember, watch the cameras," he prodded, as he left the dressing room.

Sig Eros knocked on the dressing room door and entered. "How did you end up in here?" he asked.

"Roadie Rob put us here," said Davie as he winked at Michael.

"Well it's too late to do anything now. That roadie guy is sure full of surprises. We're going to do the run through now and remember don't light that incensor."

I was glad that they had a run through, so I could see Davie in his altar boy garb, and get used to it. It was pretty hysterical, seeing my bald balladeer in his red cassock and pure white surplice. He looked more like an altar senior as he carried the crucifix around the altar. The boys were gawking around to make sure they knew where all of the cameras were located. They were joined at the altar by the divine Deaconess, my new dressing room mate. I found myself wishing that I could come across as self-assured as that full-figured young diva, with the curious habit of continually twitching and tweaking in order to reposition her underall full body girdle.

I am a second hand Catholic myself, so the meaning behind some of this ritual is lost on me. Leading the procession in was Michael with his holy water dispenser, blessing the way for the others to follow. I was always glad that Catholics didn't believe in that full body immersion stuff. I was sure that over the centuries some of the masses of Catholic women complained about ruining their outfits in the water. That little hand held sprinkler is more politically correct. Davie came next carrying the cross. He's explained that to me in the past; Christ died on the cross for Catholicism, and they need to continually remind others of that. Then Johnny Lee had to walk backward swinging the incensor at one of Roy's assistants who was standing in for the Pope. I am not sure why the head of the church would want to breathe in that foul air. Sig explained to all of them that they would have to help the Pope in going through the production, as he was not going to get a run through.

I told you about Davie having qualms of conscience about smoking pot. He decided to get rid of his remaining stash. Once the boys got back to the dressing room, Davie inconspicuously took his last two bags of pot and dumped them into the incensor which he thought was a rather harmless joke since the incensor was not to be lit. Michael filled up his sprinkler to the brim.

As the altar seniors were sitting in their dressing room there was a light knock on the door. "Ten minutes," called out this little voice.

"That must have been one of Roy's assistants," Michael surmised.

Boom, boom, boom reverberated the dressing room door as the altar boys were startled to attention.

"That could only be," started Michael as Archbishop Nelson burst through the door.

"What are you doing here?"

"We were assigned to...," said Michael.

"No, I mean why aren't you out meeting the Pope?"

"We were ...," Davie started.

"Why isn't the incensor lit?" the Archbishop continued.

"We were ...," tried Johnny Lee.

"Light that thing now!" said the Archbishop as he pointed at Davie.

Davie rolled his eyes back in his head and said, "Let God's will be done," as he lit the hashsense blend in the incensor. Then he handed it to Johnny Lee. "Amen brother, this may help you find some Pagan Babes."

"Let's get moving!" demanded Nelson.

The Pope's caravan arrived five minutes late. He was just walking in from his limousine, accompanied by Cardinal Westwood, as the Archbishop greeted him with his entourage. The University of Texas Swing Band could be heard in the background playing a rousing rendition of *The Eyes of Texas Are Upon You*. Cardinal Westwood excused himself to take his front row seats, and the Deaconess joined the party around the Pope.

In the back stage area, Sig Eros could be heard telling everyone that they were on live television and they were now five minutes behind schedule. The Archbishop was trying to make some quick introductions of all principals to the Pope.

"This is the Deacon from Rome, Texas."

"That's not a Deacon," insisted the Pope. "The church hasn't had buxom Deaconesses for a thousand years."

"Yes, I'm sure you are technically correct," said Nelson, as he talked to the one person he did not dare to steamroller. "However, this is television and your unification speech is the most important thing right now. Every country music fan in America is going to be tuned in to this program. They are all potential converts. We need this holy woman at the altar. In the American religious media business she's what's known as a hot momma holy hosanna. Even Pat Robertson does it."

"Places everyone. This is live," Sig tried.

"These are your altar boys, Johnny, Michael, and Davie Fender. He's not the annulment Fender," the Archbishop continued.

"These aren't boys, one of them is bald." stated the Pope, as the Swing Band continued playing *The Eyes of Texas Are Upon You.*

"They are The Word."

"Why are they dressed like altar men?" asked the Pope.

"We didn't have enough time to do everything. We didn't have enough time for them to play and for you to deliver the unification speech," answered the Archbishop as the incense began enveloping them in a thick mushroom cloud.

"Do you mean I'm not going to hear *Brown Eyed Handsome Cow?*" asked His Holiness.

There I was, sitting in the second row just behind Cardinal Westwood and some other dignitaries, watching my Davie procession in with the big Pope of the whole world. Michael was leading the way in with his little holy water dispenser and was delighted to give some of the notable country singers splattered through the audience a good splash. Johnny Lee was incensing the Pope as they walked to the altar. This caused a pale pink plume to cover the Pontiff who seemed to be enjoying it. I was sure I saw Davie bowing toward the smoke like a mechanical toy soldier and inhaling deeply. Everyone took their places with the boys trying to linger in the camera angles as long as possible. After reaching the altar the Pope signaled for Johnny to return and give him another prolonged blessing of Acapulco incense. And Johnny sure didn't mind being on camera longer.

Once Archbishop Nelson had shipped the Pope on stage he made a mad dash for the one place where he could take control, the control room. However, inside of the control room things were already tense. The show was now ten minutes behind schedule as His Excellency's presence back stage had caused so much excitement that they had lost another five minutes. Sig Eros was wearing his head set while standing in front of one of the control panels filled with mixers and monitors. Larry Tacoma, also wearing his head set, sat hunched over the other control panel, as he directed the swing band to wrap up the longest version ever of *the Eyes of Texas*.

Sig and Larry were a well-oiled team, having produced hundreds of shows, but none of them live. Usually they would gather two hours of uncut videotape and the maestro, Larry, would transform it into a sixty-minute sonnet.

"Why is that incensor lit? I told them a billion times not to light it," yelled Sig into the microphone on his head set. "Who told them to light it?"

Bursting through the control room door, at that very moment, was Archbishop Nelson. Sig gave him a slight glance while Larry dug his nails into the side of his panel.

"I thought I could help you gentlemen out," proclaimed the Archbishop. His offer went unaccepted as Sig adjusted the color mixers and Larry gave instructions to the cameramen.

"Keep those camera's on the Pope at all times," proclaimed the Archbishop. "And turn up the volume on that unification speech."

"You can stay if you're quiet," Larry finally stated through gritted teeth to the intruder.

"I thought you gents could benefit from my expertise."

In a nanosecond of desperation, Larry sprang onto his chair and looked down at the Archbishop. "What I meant was sit down and shut up! Shut up or I'll call security and have them drag you out of here!" he commanded.

The suddenly sheepish Archbishop found a sturdy chair and quietly sat down.

"What's with these camera shots?" asked Sig.

The Pope turned to the congregation, looked directly into camera one, and started, "I'm honored to address those of you who are here and those of you who are not all here. I'm happy, very happy to be here. I feel happier all the time," he spoke through the haze hanging over the altar, then continued on with his unification speech:

"In the beginning was the Word, and the Word was God.
And the Word was with God.
In the beginning the Word was love.
And God so loved the World, and Texas, in the beginning.
So important was the Word that I have brought The Word here tonight,
To this Garden of Austin.
The Word was in the beginning and tonight is a new beginning.
In the beginning God so loved the World that he created dark and light.
The dark he called night and gave it to the lovers, musicians and nocturnal creatures.
The light he called day and gave it to the truckers and mechanics and those over thirty.
He bad the creatures of the day to toil everlasting and to serve the creatures of the night.
God then separated the Earth into land and water.
The land he called Texas and he filled it with the most salubri..., salubrio..., healthiest of creatures.
The water he called water and he gave it to the whales, dolphins and zebra mussels.

God looked at what he had done and said it was high. And he said it was good. It was good and high."

The Pope motioned Johnny Lee to approach and resume incensing. As Johnny complied the entire altar was engulfed in a purple haze. As the Pope continued his unification speech, he was little more than a Felliniesque silhouette on millions of television screens around the world:

"God said all that I have done is good,

But life would be barren without music.

God said let there be sound.

He placed the birds in the sky, and told them to sing.

He placed the wind in the air and told it to blow.

God placed the thunder in the heavens and told it to clap.

He placed some corn into a horn 'til it was born.

He dained that all of his creatures have rock 'n roll, the rhythm method, and ragtime.

God brought together the lovers, the songwriters, and the musicians.

He bad them to mingle with the stars of night

Out high and bright, deep in the heart of Texas.

All was good.

God was happy.

I am happy.

God was merry.

I am very merry.

He gave the songwriters melody and modulation.

God said there shall be music throughout the land.

The music shall be of one with the country.

The music shall be of the country.

The music shall be for the country.

For all eternity it shall be known as country music.

God took the wood from the trees and made the fiddle.

He took the silk from the worms and made strings.

He took the orchestration and syncopation of nature and created the grand operatic gift of country music.

Country music begat Vernon Dahlman, who begat Jimmie Rogers, who begat Bill Monroe and The Bluegrass Boys. Bluegrass begat Flatt and Scruggs, who begat Roy Acuff, who begat Pee Wee King, who ultimately begat Elvis."

In the control room the show had begat one huge headache for Sig and Larry as they hunched over their control boards.

"What the hell is going on with all of this incense? There is nothing in the script about all of these extra trips to the altar," Sig fumed. "Look at these monitors. I can barely see the Pope for all of this damn smoke."

"Holy Smoke!" said Nelson.

"It's going to set off the smoke alarms and the sprinkler system if we can't clear it out. Call maintenance and see if they can't speed up the air exchanger," Sig continued. He was already showing large blotches of sweat coming through his shirt. Larry picked up the phone to call maintenance.

"Maybe I can take charge of the smoke," Archbishop Nelson tried.

Larry moved the phone away from his mouth and held up his other finger over his lips like a parent shushing a child.

The Archbishop slumped back into his chair showing a look of childhood rejection.

Larry hung up the phone and reported to Sig, "They're doing everything that they can. The auxiliary air exchanger hasn't worked for two years. They've opened some outside doors, but they're afraid of ending up with a mess of bats in here."

"What bats would want to breathe this?" said Sig.

"This is why we don't do live TV," added Larry tersely as he peered at the Archbishop.

"I prefer bats to the Austin Fire Department, especially in the middle of a show," said Sig.

The phone in the control room rang. Sig picked it up and listened. "Yes Porter, I know we are running twelve minutes late. I know the auditorium is full of smoke. You're the one that made the deal with the devil about doing a live show. If you want to help, go open a couple more doors and keep the bats out. I need to keep this phone open. Don't call back," Sig spouted as he threw down the phone.

"We're twelve minutes late without any way to make it up. Does the Pope know the rest of the script?" Sig asked.

The Archbishop sprung to his feet seeing an opportunity. "I'll forget that deal with the devil remark. I have given the Pope the full benefit of my knowledge. We reviewed the script several times," he said.

"He looks wobbly to me," said Larry. "I think that smoke is depriving him of oxygen."

"He was slurring some words toward the end of his speech. Does he remember, no communion for the audience?" added Sig.

The Archbishop had moved himself in-between the other two men. "The Pope knows the plan better than I do," he said.

"Yes, the plan," said Larry as he pointed toward the Archbishop's chair.

Sig picked up the phone and punched a number. "Tell that roadie Rob to go out to the altar and get the incense away from that pyromaniac."

"Michael Vaughn," said the Archbishop from his chair.

Sig and Larry exchanged glances as Sig continued on the phone. "What do you mean, he's not there. Then you go out there and get that incensor. Take it away from him," Sig said. "I don't care if he puts up a fight. You won't be on camera anyway."

He put down the phone and spoke into his headset, "Camera one stay tight on the Pope. Camera two get a close up on the Deaconess. Camera three scan the audience away from the guy with the incense. All cameras stay away from the incense."

Back at the altar, the Pope was continuing his promise to bring more country music masses to Catholic Americans. He laboriously thanked every American who had assisted him during this trip. Off to his left, His Holiness spotted the stage hand trying to take the incensor away from Johnny Lee and stopped his monologue. "Sir, we'll be needing that for the rest of the service," he said. Directing a quick comment to Johnny Lee, the blushing back stager scampered off.

"Hold those shots, hold those shots," cried Sig into his headset, as the world watched the delectable Deaconess twitching and tugging.

Johnny Lee went to the altar and whispered into the Pope's ear. Johnny was making sweeping gestures creating a disco strobe effect through the cumulus clouds. His Holiness agreed with him. Johnny turned and incensed the Pope, then departed the altar. On his way out he stopped and gave Davie some personal puffs of incense that were followed by a big wink. Johnny Lee and the smoke bomb disappeared back stage.

In a resonant melodious Gregorian chant, His Holiness sang out, "Glo-o-o-o-r-ia." He was immediately accompanied by the meliferous Deaconess singing harmony, and the swing band filling in softly behind them as they finished the *Gloria in Excelsis Deo*.

"Let us all rise and begin the celebration of God's greatest gift," intoned His Holiness, signaling the beginning of the High Mass, as if anyone needed to get higher.

The Deaconess immediately began pointing and telling the boys what to do and where to go in order to be proper altar guys.

In his low rich resonant tone, the Pope chanted, "In nominee Patris et Filii et Spiritus Sancti, Amen."

"Ad Deum qui laetificat juventutem mean," answered the divine Deaconess in her own golden modulation.

"Dominus Vobiscum," the Pope continued.

"Et cum Spiritu tuo," she answered, with just a minor tug of adjustment.

As the Deaconess directed them around the altar Davie remembered some of the modus operandi, but poor Michael was lost. He had never been an altar boy before. Actually, he had never been a Catholic before. For the washing and drying of the Pope's hands, Davie took the diminutive crystal cruets and Michael took the embroidered linen towel. After Davie washed His Holiness' hands, Michael tried to dry them, until the Pope finally wrestled the towel away from Michael.

Finally, there was some favorable news in the control room. The purple haze of the past was now pink mist and dissipating quickly.

"I told you it would be a great show," added the Archbishop, as Johnny Lee returned to the stage without the incense.

"We've got to get through communion first," answered Sig.

On cue and on time, The Pope held up a large host over his head. "I present to you the holy Eucharist, the body and blood of our Lord Jesus Christ," he proclaimed as he gave the Deaconess and the former band members shares of the host.

"Amen."

The Pope extended his arms in a gesture of peace. "Let us all join in, Gloria Patri et Filio et Spiritui Sancto," he chanted, as he removed the chalice veil from a magnificent magnum of wine.

"What is that? What is that?" stammered Larry.

"Sacrificial wine," answered the Archbishop.

"Where are the tiny cruets?" asked Larry

"I thought only Gallo came in bottles that big," said Sig, as the Pope invited the Deaconess and the altar men to the altar.

His Excellency gave the Deaconess a blessing and then handed her the chalice full of wine as she tried to balance the chalice and shimmy her undergarments into place. The Pope continued to chat with the Deaconess and observed her sporadic gyrations. He apparently assumed that her adjustments were physical manifestations of a deep seeded worship moment. His Holiness whispered to the Deaconess, "I am so pleased that my presence has caused the spirit of the Father, Son and Holy Ghost to surge through your soul in such an obvious biomagnetic demonstration." The Pope then poured sacrificial wine for the altar men and finally himself. After all had partaken in the wine for the first time the Pope cleansed the chalice. He then poured his altar mates a second goblet of wine. Johnny approached His Holiness and was telling him something. I dreaded he was asking for that list of pagan babies. He then pointed toward the swing band and the Pope seemed to be agreeing with him about something.

"Hell's bells, this is boring," blurted out Larry. "I can hear TV sets clicking off all over the land. Who wants to watch four old men drinking wine?"

"That's the Pope," said Archbishop Nelson, showing Larry he wasn't going to be totally quiet.

"Larry it's almost over. After they finish communion, the Pope blesses the women and they parade out," Sig reassured his good buddy. "We are thirteen minutes over, but nothing more can go wrong now."

At the altar, Johnny Lee was telling the Pope something and pointing at Davie. I was hoping that this would be the moment of the plenary indulgence. The Pope then signaled for Michael to bring him the holy water. His Holiness took the holy water from Michael and handed it to the Deaconess. To the left of the altar Michael and Johnny Lee huddled briefly. I felt sure that the Pope would have Davie step forward and get his blessing.

"In the name of the Father and the Son and the Holy Spirit," started the Pope as three bats swooped from the darkness into the spotlights. The audience produced a simultaneous shriek and the bats retreated into the rafters. "After a nationwide search we have identified three women of such felicity and purity that we honor them today," the Pope continued. "They are Gloria Spears, Fran Eros, and Marion Hensley. Please stand." That was fast. I was sitting there thinking that Davie was going to get his absolution. Then bam, I was being blessed on national television. Nervous me.

"These women are just the tip of the iceberg," His Holiness continued. They represent millions of good Christian women who keep their moralistic force under water. The church has a place for all women, and we want all women to know their places. The church is ready to turn up the heat and thaw these women so they may assume their positions as country western Catholics." He then took the holy water from the Deaconess and walked to the edge of the altar. He sprinkled in our direction, drenching Cardinal Westwood but leaving us unaffected, except for Gloria whom almost swallowed her gum.

Michael had slipped backstage under the cover of bats and icebergs. Attempting to walk in his most sanctimonious manner, he was returning to the altar along with his guitar and Davie's fiddle. Johnny Lee went to the piano and nudged the swing band pianist off of his perch. He twitched a hitch in his get along, pushed the bench aside and stood there playing some hot honky tonk piano. "I said come on Texans," Johnny wailed. "We got prayin' going on, on, on. Come on Texans, you know you can't go wrong, wrong ,wrong. We ain't strayin', whole lota prayin' going on." He had that piano dancing. "We got prayin' in Austin, not Austin, yes Austin. We got prayin' in Austin, Austin, Austin. Come on Texans, whole lotta prayin' going on."

At the center of the altar, eyes twinkling and facing the congregation, the Pope clapped in time to the music.

Suddenly for Davie it was the Riverside Ballroom thirty years earlier. He and that non-native Johnny Lee were competing for the hearts and souls of the Bay's bobby soxers. This time there would be no doubt about who was the best performer. He started in with his flaming fiddle, flouncing around under his bulky cassock and perfectly hitting his licks. Michael followed on guitar as the bats began swooping down in time to the music.

Raising both hands up over her head the Deaconess exhorted the uptempo audience, "Come on Texans whole lotta prayin' going on, on, on."

Johnny Lee and his torching piano continued, "We got prayin' in Austin, Austin, Austin. Come on Texans whole lotta prayin' going on. Let's pray it people pray. I said pray it people pray. Let's pray it pagans pray. I said pray it pagans pray. Ain't strayin', whole lota prayin' going on," as the crowd clapped with uninhibited exultation, and Gloria enthusiastically crackled her gum in my ear.

Davie's style was being entangled by his billowy cassock. He took the front of the skirt and tucked it into his blue jeans, showing off his Grateful Dead buckle. My bald buckaroo pranced a complete circle around the altar. Knees high. His fiddle was sizzling. Let's see Johnny Lee do that, he thought, as the audience ahhed his performance. Their energy swept the intoxicated audience like wild fire.

"We got prayin' in the church. Who's church? My church. Really got the devil by the horns," Johnny continued singing as everyone stood and stomped. "Come on over people we got prayin' in the church. Who's church? My church. Our church. Come on over pagans whole lotta prayin' going on."

I felt totally fulfilled.

"Bring it down now," Johnny sung. Making his voice softer and tinkling the high notes, he continued, "We got praying going on, on, on." Then softer, "Come on over Texans, we got prayin' going on, on, on." Then Johnny, accompanied by the audience, "Come on over Texans, we got prayin' going on, on, on. Come on over Texans, we got..."

In the control room there was abundant prayin' going on. "What is this? What is this?" Larry yelled, as Sig pounded his head without missing a beat.

"This is all wrong!" Larry protested.

"You're right. He's not the piano player," said the Archbishop.

"No, he's an altar boy," Sig said.

"No, the bald guy is the piano player," Nelson countered.

"None of them are piano players. They're altar boys," Larry tried.

"Well, it's not boring," affirmed the Archbishop.

"It's not in the script either. And the Pope, that you prepared so well, is going along with it," stated the peevish Larry as the control room phone began ringing.

Immediately Johnny Lee launched into *When The Saints Go Marching In*. "Well I want to be in that number when the saints go marching in," he was singing while demonstrating his keyboard mastery.

Symphoniously swinging his arms, His Holiness was conducting a good old Catholic revival. The young collegians in the swing band were way too willing and immediately joined in.

"Oh when the saints, oh when the saints, oh when the saints go marching in," trilled the Deaconess, as she encouraged a ready crowd. Fortissimo.

"Yes, we want to be in that number, when the saints go marching in," responded the studio audience.

My country star was ready to make another statement as he bolted from the stage and fiddled in the aisles. As he started strutting up the aisle, Gloria Spears bolted from her special post and sprinted toward my Davie with an admiring look that exceeded good old fashion Christian ardor. She began following him and fortunately dozens of others in the rock 'n holy congregation followed her. He went up one aisle and down another as the numbers in his procession increased. When he paraded by our location I grabbed Gloria by the arm and pulled her back to her seat.

"Remember, you're a special woman," I told her.

"Oh my saints, what a man," she gushed in heavy breath.

"Find your own man," I demanded, realizing that I hadn't given anyone a smack in the kisser for a very long time.

"Oh when the saints go marching in," filled the studio. Half of the audience was following Davie and singing in celebration, "Lord I want to be in that number when the saints go marching in."

Having borrowed a tuba from the swing band, Michael was trailing the snake line showing off his marching band moves. The Word was so busy strutting their stuff that they failed to notice that Roy Ryman was about to get into the act. From the rear of the studio came the perennial promoter, with three conscripts, carrying a long banner with bright bold letters. Through the aisles they were carrying a peppy tempera banner that proclaimed, THE HOWLING DOG SALOON, GREEN

BAY, WIS. Marching in time, they continued until they had gone past the swing band and over the stage. Some in the startled studio audience were applauding the banner as others were singing, "Oh Lord I want to shout hallelujah, when the saints go marching in."

"I told you they were tuba players," yelled Larry.

"Why are all of these cameras on that banner?" demanded Sig. "Camera one, back on the Pope. Camera two on the Deaconess," he concluded, only to see that both cameras were following the progress of the banner, as the congregation finished singing.

"One last time. Well I want to be in that number, when the saints go marching in.," Johnny concluded, as the banner went out of sight.

Back in Wisconsin, Sister Mary Lynn was standing in front of her set, little droplets running down her cheeks, and singing along. Total jubilation.

The celebration in the studio began to calm as His Holiness huddled with his team.

Regal looking and restrained, the Pope raised his arms as the crowd quieted some and returned to their seats. "Amen," he said.

"Amen!" was returned even though the audience was still buzzing.

"Good," said Sig.

"Children of God, we have one more offering for you today," said the Pope.

"Damn," said Sig. "I thought Amen meant the end."

"Not always," said the Archbishop. "I hope they do *Brown Eyed Handsome Cow*."

Johnny had begun caressing the keys and the band followed.

"Amazing grace how sweet the sound that saved a wretch like me," sang the vigorous Holy Father as he signaled the Deaconess to join him at the altar. Together they sang, "How sweet the sound."

"That saved a wretch like me," began the congregation as a single bat flitted in and out of the spotlights.

Michael and Davie slipped in behind them singing harmony, "I once was lost but now I'm found, was blind, but now I see."

Now back on their feet, the audience swayed with the melody. Davie motioned to me. In an instant, this bashful baritone was standing with the other four at the altar and singing, "Thru many dangers, toils and snares I have already come."

The teary eyed assemblage enclosed in one large womb was moving to the music. And Davie was heard singing above the crowd, "Tis grace has brought me safe thus far. And grace will lead me home."

Davie peered to the back of the auditorium and saw an uncommonly distinguished looking being who was watching him intently. He was immediately taken with this personage, obviously important, but so short in stature. This holy soul that Davie thought he saw presented an aura of everlasting tranquillity that my man could almost reach out and touch. He told me later, that it was at that moment he felt a warm hug of well being as if a messenger was telling him 'Everything will be okay'.

Sister Mary Lynn, still standing in her living room, was singing along, "The Lord has promised good to me. His word my hope secures."

Never had I felt so interconnected. To the galaxies. To every grain of sand.

Even in the control room, Sig and Larry joined in, "He will my shield and portion be as long as life endures."

The Deaconess gestured to the orchestra for a wrap then raised her arms to the audience as they reluctantly brought the song to a close.

"God bless you. Love one another. Go in peace," said His Holiness. And with that he turned and headed directly out of the building.

In the control room, Sig was drenched but feeling faintly victorious. Larry sprang onto his chair yelling, "Holy special! I smell holy special!"

"I told you so," boomed the Archbishop over his shoulder as he ran to catch the Pope's motorcade.

Chapter Eighteen
Benediction
Austin, Texas

The crowds were gone and the studio was empty. Davie and I were lingering on the dimly lit stage.

"Nothing is quieter than an empty auditorium after a performance," he said. "A building struck dumb, and the melodies playing only in our memories."

"I was so proud of you," I said. "Helen and Otto would have been proud of you too."

"Maybe Ford will underwrite the show. That would really make my old man proud. Marion I'm just happy that you're happy. I didn't talk to the Pope, but that's not important now. I'm at peace with myself."

There we stood at center stage where the altar had just been removed. I got him a folding chair and kissed the top of his glistening head as he sat down. He consciously pulled himself upright on the slick metal surface of the chair.

"I'm going back stage," I said, knowing that he would like a few moments to reflect on the evening. The door clicked behind me as I left the empty auditorium.

Davie pointed toward the back and then at the aisles as he remembered Roy parading around with his banner. He blinked his eyes and stared into the darkness wondering if he'd really seen someone in the back of hall. Slowly gazing from seat to seat he remembered who had been sitting where as the studio door clicked again. He heard firm foot steps behind him that then stopped at the piano and someone tinkled the keys. It must be him he thought, then turned to see Johnny Lee.

"You're the man, Davie," Johnny said. "You were the best performer on stage tonight," he continued as they shook hands.

"Thanks, Johnny. That means a lot coming from you. I don't even care if it's all a bunch of bull, I'll take it."

"You were the one that got us here. Somehow. Sometimes the greatest gifts come from the least likely places."

"I'm sorry about the Pagan Babies," Davie said.

"I can't look for the pagans to save me. I have to save myself."

Davie brought himself up ramrod straight and pulled his shoulders back. "You know I used to be a slouch. But now that life itself is being taken away I feel the need to show my strength."

"You'll understand if I don't come to your funeral. I'll be back in Atlanta trying to Fenderize my life."

"I don't think you want to go that far."

"Say hi to Scott Joplin for me," said Johnny as he clamped onto Davie's hand and they shook for the last time.

Tinkle, tinkle, click, click, and Johnny was gone.

Davie inhaled slowly and gazed into the solitude as the studio door clicked again. After some clunking around, the

Deaconess appeared out of the dim carrying another folding chair.

"Reckon it would be all right for me to join you?" she asked.

"How could I say no to the woman that broke a thousand years of church tradition."

As she situated her chair they heard the whooshing of some bats in the rafters. "What is that?" she asked.

"It's either a sign from God, or bats in the catwalk."

"I choose to believe it's bats. I don't know what message God would have for us after leading the Pope into a revival session."

"He seemed to be enjoying himself. I'll bet he's inking a deal with RCA right now," Davie concluded. He looked intently at the Deaconess and asked, "Did you see a remarkably distinguished looking person standing in the back? Rather short."

"No Davie, I didn't. Was it Andrew Lloyd Weber? Maybe he wants to take this to Broadway."

"I don't think so."

"You wanted a plenary indulgence didn't you?"

"I did, but now I know everything is going to be all right."

Reaching over and taking Davie's hand, the Deaconess said, "Our father who art in Heaven, I recommend this soul into eternal salvation. Amen."

"Amen," he said. "My life is down to seeds and stems."

"I know you've planted many good seeds," she said as she stood to leave. "Say hi to Patsy Cline for me. I just love her to death," she finished and slowly released his hand.

Davie again pulled himself upright in his chair as the Deaconess left the studio. Click, click.

Click, click. I was hoping that he had mused enough so I returned. "Are you ready to go home cowboy?"

"I'm sure 'nuff ready to go anywhere with you ma'am."

Chapter Nineteen
October 18, 1998
Green Bay, Wisconsin

That final farewell at The Howling Dog was almost too much for me. For the occasion Davie, Michael and I had crafted a home made video and Roy had hired three bands. I had spent a week putting together my outfit, which was inspired by a black gaucho hat I found while going through Davie's things. After a dozen stops, I found matching patent leather boots at Lou's Boot Barn. Then, I had to go to Appleton, of all places, to find a raven-colored western skirt and matching blouse.

If Michael and his wife Valerie hadn't picked me up that night, I'd still be sitting at the apartment. When we walked into The Dog's door all conversation stopped. I could feel all eyes fixed on me. Somehow, I knew instinctively what to do. I walked promptly to the microphone even though things were pretty much a blur. Later, I realized there was a standing room crowd. I thanked them for coming and told them not to be sad. I said it was a special night for me and I hoped it would be special for them. Davie was all about having fun and tonight we were going to have fun. I could feel tears running down my cheeks as I spoke, but I really didn't care. All of those people came to pay tribute to Davie and I was going to thank them, no matter what. I managed to mention Roy and his generosity in hosting this tribute, but that was as much as I could say. Fortunately, Roy had saved my place at the bar. As I walked to my stool, I ran right into the ever buoyant Sister Lynn perched on a stool of her own. She gave me a huge hug. A nun at The Howling Dog, that must have been a first.

Michael then stepped to the microphone. "Davie wanted you all to enjoy yourselves tonight, and thus he contributed his life savings. I believe that was about a dollar ninety eight."

Michael then explained about the souvenir dolls that were for sale. They were miniature Davies complete with bow and fiddle. The doll was bald except for several strands of a ponytail made from real hair. Roy promised to donate all of the profits from the dolls to Sister Mary Lynn's day care program.

Finally he announced, "Now please direct your attention to the TV monitors around the room."

I felt relieved. A chance to laugh through my tears. Naturally Davie was the inspiration for the farewell video. He was weak when we worked on the video, but we had fun making it. His fertile mind never stopped oozing; he was an artist to the end.

The scene opened with a view of a wooden structure. Then the camera zoomed in on four pieces of ordinary notebook paper each painted with an individual oriental symbol. Davie had found the Japanese words expressing the four seasons and wanted them to be part of the drama. The camera went to a wider angle and there I was standing in front of this weathered building. They had me dressed up in a dark blue blazer and matching skirt. It had wide lapels and golden captain's buttons. It was supposed to be dated, yet professional.

"Hello my name is Carla Phillips and I'm here today with Professor Pearson at the Willmet Farm in Grove Mills, Wisconsin. We have discovered what we believe to be a flying saucer from Mars. The professor has gone aboard. Let's get a closer look at the saucer."

The camera came in tight on the rustic wooden door. The crowd was totally silent, looking back and forth from me to the woman in the video. The camera panned back and the wooden building was recognizable as an outhouse. The door opened slowly and out stepped Davie. He was wearing a sports coat, tie and blue jeans. He had decided not to wear a hat, and some gasped when they saw him. The effect was great; many of his fans had not seen him sans hair. Thankfully, I could start to see some glimmer of understanding on their faces.

He began to speak, "I'm Professor Pearson from U.W. - Green Bay."

Finally a little laugh of recognition from the fans. He continued, "I'm here to report to you about some little green men that have come to take me to the other side. I'd introduce them to you, but they are inside eating some of our finest Wisconsin products: green cheese and green bratwursts."

The audience seemed to be relaxing some and started getting into it.

"They asked me to shave. Seems I got a little carried away." Davie said as he stroked his head. "We have a few more minutes until blast off. While we wait, Marion and I would like to sing a little song for you."

Davie and I sang one of our favorite songs, *I Was Made For You And You Were Made For Me*. We did it as a duet, even though it wasn't originally a duet. We altered the lyrics a little, added some stuff about our lives together, and ended with Davie losing his battle with cancer. My memory of the evening gets pretty fuzzy after that.

At the end of our song Davie gave me a hug and showstopper kiss, that was way too short for me. I wanted to be entwined with my cowboy forever. He held my hand up toward the camera in order to show off my wedding ring and gave me another big hug and kiss.

Davie continued. "Don't feel sorry for me. I had every advantage in life. Maybe too many advantages. I even met the Pope once, but that's another story. By the time you see this I'll be a strumming with Hank and Gram and the boys." Davie repositioned his guitar. "Here's my final number.

"Traded in my old life of mirth,
Just praying with the holy church.
Sitting on my pastor's knee,
Counting blessings one, two, three.

I am headed to the other side,
Singing with the Lord's joyous tide.
Sitting on St. Peter's knee,
Counting halos one, two, three.

Life was holey, life was great,
But I am bound to Heaven's gate.
Sitting on my maker's knee,
Shouting all ye oxen, come in free.

Life is fun if you fiddle.
Life ain't nothing but a holey holy riddle."

The camera panned back and Davie handed me his guitar. He then walked into the outhouse and waved out the door.

Davie had this idea of towing this outhouse for a few feet with his Tempo in order to simulate the space ship taking off. We had a momentary pause in the videotape while Davie slipped out the door and they repositioned the rope. Then action. The sound of Davie's rat-a-tat Tempo engine could be heard on the tape, adding more drama than we had imagined. The rope became taut, and the decrepit old building started to move. Then the rope tightened too much. Suddenly, the structure exploded into a thousand splinters. There was weathered wood everywhere. Rustic boards shooting and falling. Clouds of gray decaying kindling. The sawdust finally settled and the camera refocused on a three hole seat that had survived the disintegration. Out of the middle hole an arm appeared, and Davie waved his last good bye.

Order Form
Life Ain't Nothing But a
Holey Holy Riddle

Name:_____

Address:_____

_____

Phone: _____

_____# of books at $12.00 each; total:_____

postage and handling $2.00 per book; total:_____

Total enclosed:_____

Make checks payable to John Polodna. Please do not send cash.

Mail the order to

**Polodna Publishing
2440 Markridge Circle
Racine, Wisconsin 53405 - 1449**